THE GUILD CODEX: WARPED / ONE

WARPING MINDS & OTHER MISDEMEANORS

ANNETTE MARIE
ROB JACOBSEN

Warping Minds & Other Misdemeanors
The Guild Codex: Warped / Book One
By Annette Marie & Rob Jacobsen

Dark Owl Fantasy Inc.
PO Box 88106, Rabbit Hill Post Office
Edmonton, AB, Canada T6R 0M5
www.darkowlfantasy.com

Cover Copyright © 2020 by Annette Ahner
Cover and Book Interior by Midnight Whimsy Designs
www.midnightwhimsydesigns.com

Editing by Elizabeth Darkley
arrowheadediting.wordpress.com

ISBN 978-1-988153-55-1

MORE BOOKS BY ANNETTE MARIE

STEEL & STONE UNIVERSE

Steel & Stone Series
Chase the Dark
Bind the Soul
Yield the Night
Reap the Shadows
Unleash the Storm
Steel & Stone

Spell Weaver Trilogy
The Night Realm
The Shadow Weave
The Blood Curse

OTHER WORKS

Red Winter Trilogy
Red Winter
Dark Tempest
Immortal Fire

THE GUILD CODEX

CLASSES OF MAGIC

Spiritalis

Psychica

Arcana

Demonica

Elementaria

MYTHIC

A person with magical ability

MPD / MAGIPOL

The organization that regulates mythics and their activities

ROGUE

A mythic living in violation of MPD laws

MAGICAE POLITIAE
DENUNTIATORES
MPD

WARPING MINDS
& OTHER MISDEMEANORS

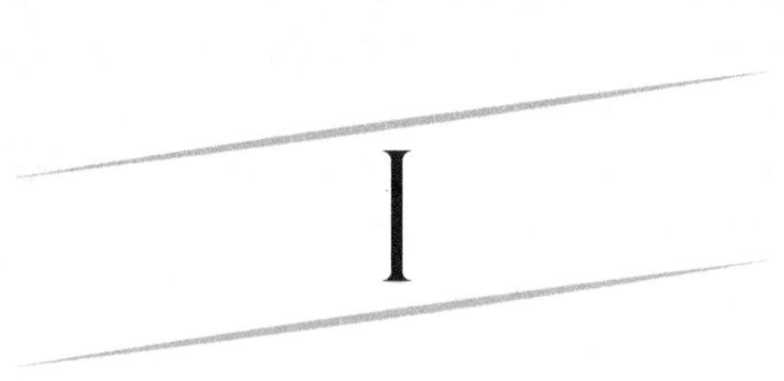

I

I'M NOT GONNA LIE. Being restrained by handcuffs in a room with two powerful, beautiful women has a certain appeal. However, when those two women are cops and the room is a cold, barren box used for interrogations, the allure diminishes dramatically.

Captain Blythe dropped a stack of folders on the metal table with a loud *smack*, rattling the chains that ran from the tabletop to my wrists. She settled into the seat across from me and pushed up the sleeves of her simple white blouse. With wavy blond hair to her shoulders and cheekbones to spare, she had a kind of Cate Blanchett thing going on. Minus the charm. Or the accent.

"Kit Morris." Her blue-eyed stare scraped like icicles. "Tell me everything you know."

"Everything?" Did she mean that literally? I glanced at the second woman in the room for a clue.

Agent Lienna Shen. While Blythe had the *Men in Black* look down, Lienna might've wandered into the precinct by accident. Just shy of five and a half feet tall, she'd covered her simple blue-jeans-and-black-jacket outfit in knickknacks—leather bracelets, beads hanging from her ponytail of thick raven hair, silver rings on her slender fingers, chains and necklaces layered over her white t-shirt, and a hemp satchel slung over one shoulder.

When she caught me looking her way, she added a well-honed scowl to her accessories list.

Since neither woman was offering an explanation, I shrugged. "That could take a while. I know a lot of things. For example, the brachiosaur sounds in *Jurassic Park* were made by mixing whale and donkey noises together."

Blythe's eyes squinched. "What?"

"You said you wanted everything. I'm a bit of a movie buff, so I know lots of film trivia."

"Do not screw with me," she growled—and for a split second, both the table and my chair lifted off the floor.

The table and I hovered for a second, then dropped. My chair hit the linoleum, then my tailbone hit the chair. The impact jarred my teeth, the bang of the table landing ringing in my ears.

Oh, fun. Blythe was a telekinetic. And angry.

The captain leaned across the table. "Don't forget where you are. This isn't a TV show. We aren't the police. You don't get a phone call or a lawyer. This is the MPD, and in this precinct, you are completely, unalterably at my mercy. Do you understand?"

I nodded, playing it cool despite the dour voice in my head tallying all the ways in which I was completely screwed. My gaze darted away from her menacing glare and landed on my warped reflection in the one-way mirror behind her. It made me look like a deranged GI Joe doll.

To be fair, I hadn't showered or shaved since my arrest two days prior, and this dull gray jumpsuit wasn't doing my summer tan any favors—though it sure made my baby blues pop. But considering a very generous barista had once compared me to a young Chris Pine, the hobo-soldier look was depressing.

Blythe flipped a folder open. "We're on our third interview, Mr. Morris, and I have no patience left. It'd be in your best interest to change your attitude before this session is over."

Was that a threat? I'd liked her initial strategy better: the classic interrogation method where she'd started out considerate and conversational, offered me a hot drink and a snack, then subtly manipulated me into revealing self-incriminating tidbits about my past—or she'd tried. Maybe I should've been less obvious about deflecting her questions.

Not to say she was bad at her job, but this wasn't my first interrogation.

I slouched back in my chair. "What do you want to know?"

"I want answers about your guild, Kirk, Conner & Qasid. *Real* answers." She picked up a pen. "How long were you a member of KCQ?"

"About a year before shit hit the fan."

"And the same night your guild fell, you attempted to flee the country?" Her tone suggested she didn't think much of my bid to secure basic, prison-free survival.

"I *did* flee the country," I corrected. "And I would've fled the continent too, but I didn't expect MagiPol to send a superstar sorcerer after me."

I gestured to Lienna, chains jangling unpleasantly. She maintained her scowl. Damn, her poker face was good. My previous interrogations had featured Blythe alone, so when Lienna had shown up for this one, I'd hoped for the timeless good cop/bad cop routine, but that didn't seem to be happening.

"What was your role in KCQ?" Blythe asked.

"Support for the lawyers at the firm," I answered promptly.

Blythe jotted that down. "What kind of support?"

"Emotional."

The captain raised an unimpressed eyebrow. "Emotional."

"Well, yeah. Literally." When she continued to stare expectantly, I added, "Me and another guy handled it. The lawyers would tell us what state of mind they needed their client in, and we'd come up with a way to get them there."

"So, by *support*, you mean *manipulation*."

I shrugged. "I like to think of it as emotional guidance."

"And how did you 'emotionally guide' clients?"

"I'm not sure how to describe it."

A phone beeped imperiously, but she ignored it. "Did you use magic?"

"Who said I have magic?"

The phone beeped again. Blythe sighed, reached under the table, and lifted a cell phone into view. The screen lit up as she checked her messages. Her mouth tightened, which I took to mean doom and disaster were impending and we should take shelter immediately.

Standing, she clipped the phone back to her belt and turned to Lienna. "I need to take care of something. Keep him talking."

"Yes, ma'am."

With a sharp nod, Blythe strode out of the room and graciously slammed the door behind her.

"A little intense, isn't she?" I observed.

Lienna took the vacated seat. "She's a precinct captain in one of the biggest cities in the country."

Hmm. Despite her neutral tone, her voice had a soft, caressing quality that I found surprisingly pleasant. It was a shame she wasn't playing good cop.

"Every day, Captain Blythe deals with rampant magic, illicit guilds, arrogant guild masters who think they're above the law, and violent criminals who use their abilities to hurt, cheat, or kill people."

She didn't add, "Violent criminals *just like you*." Her restraint impressed me.

"And," she continued, "all while keeping the existence of magic, guilds, and the MPD hidden from the public. A crucial mandate your guild flouted." She cleared her throat. "But you were just an intern, weren't you, Kit? You were doing what you were told. You don't need to protect them."

I grinned. "That works better without the throat-clear first. Really obvious tell that you're about to bullshit me, I've gotta say."

She stiffened in her seat.

"Oh, and try to relax more. The fake sympathy will be more convincing."

Her glower returned full force, obliterating the remnants of her kind expression. It'd been a decent attempt at building a rapport with me. She wasn't experienced at the technique, which seemed like an oversight in her training, but I suspected Lienna's real role in the agency involved far more skill than mere interrogation.

According to the rumors floating through the holding cells—of which I believed maybe five percent—Agent Lienna Shen was an abjuration sorcerer, and abjuration was … anti-magic sorcery?

That concluded my knowledge on the topic. But I *did* know the handcuffs around my wrists were an artifact created by a sorcerer for a specific magical purpose: in this case, nullifying the magic of whoever had the unfortunate pleasure of wearing them.

When she didn't respond to my helpful critique, I attempted a charming smile. "You're pretty young for an agent."

Lienna's scowl deepened, even though it was a reasonable observation; she looked my age, which seemed like a stretch for full agenthood.

"Do you know why you're here?" she asked coldly. "In this room?"

"Because Blythe has a thing for younger guys who can quote the entire courtroom speech from *A Few Good Men?*"

"Because," she said in that clipped tone people use when they're silently praying for patience—or imagining what it'd feel like to strangle me, "we're currently investigating three cases of extortion totaling two million dollars, five cases of embezzlement over five hundred thousand dollars *each*, and eight reports of blackmail. Your guild was behind them all, and unless you want those charges added to your already extensive list of crimes, you should *strongly* consider shedding some light on the inner workings of KCQ."

Despite myself, my mood sobered. This wasn't my first interrogation, but it *was* my first time in the custody of the international organization responsible for dispatching magic-wielding criminals. I had no idea what to expect as far as charges and sentencing.

"Let's go back to the beginning," she suggested. "Your name."

"Kit Morris."

"How old are you?"

"Twenty-two."

"What's your magic class?"

"Psychica." Which she already knew. KCQ had been a guild populated entirely by voodoo-brain psychics with wildly varying abilities—all the wilder once I'd joined the team.

She checked the notes in the folder. "Why aren't you registered?"

"Should I be?" I asked innocently.

"Every mythic is legally required to be registered, but we have no record of you. We didn't know you existed until we took your friend, Quentin, into custody."

I feigned dismay. "He gave me up?"

Her expression remained painfully impartial. "Why aren't you registered?"

"I didn't even know being registered was a thing until last year." I tilted my head thoughtfully. "No one at KCQ ever mentioned how it's done."

Nor had they suggested I go ahead and list myself in the mythic database for the MPD to see. Who was surprised?

"Why didn't your parents register you when your abilities manifested?"

"I never knew my parents."

It wasn't a big deal. Not to me, at least. It was just a fact. The sky is blue, Meryl Streep is the greatest living actor, and Kit Morris is an orphan.

Her eyes widened in surprise, then softened—for real this time. She still despised me, but now she felt sorry for me too, which, in my opinion, was worse.

I expected her to offer one of those lame non-apologies that people mumble when they find out your life is more tragic than theirs, but all she managed was a quiet, "Oh," before making a note in the folder. Probably something like, "Bad criminal because orphaned," with a sad face doodled beside it.

She set the pen down and folded her hands together. "Let's talk about your magic. When did you learn you were a mythic?"

Her question stalled me. Was she asking when I'd first realized I had a supernatural ability, or when I'd first learned "mythic" was the most common term for a magic user and that it applied to me?

Since my answer to the first was way less specific than the second, I went with that one. "I always knew I was different, I guess. I realized early on I could do things that scared the people around me."

"What sort of things?"

"Like I told your boss, it's difficult to describe."

"Try."

"Or," I drawled, giving her a wink, "I could give you a demonstration."

And her glare was back. "Not a chance."

I'm an overall likable guy—unless you're a soulless crumpet who loathes pop culture, in which case I'm your worst nightmare—but Lienna and I had gotten off on the wrong foot. Our first flirtatious encounter had involved her tackling me to the floor six steps away from Gate 134 at the Los Angeles airport. If not for her Marshawn Lynch impersonation, I'd be tanning on a tropical beach.

Instead, she'd arrested me, marched me onto a plane headed right back to Vancouver, and escorted me straight into Blythe's coldly welcoming arms.

I gloomily jangled my cuffs again.

Lienna poised her pen above the folder. "Please describe your magic."

"A demonstration is really the only way. What if I promise to be good?"

"You expect me to trust you?"

I nodded toward the satchel hanging off her shoulder. "I'm sure you have plenty of fun and exciting toys in that bag to keep me in check if I misbehave."

"I'm not stupid, Kit," she snapped, that soft note I liked in her voice vanishing. "Don't try to play me."

Her tone rubbed me the wrong way. "If you're so smart, why are you just an agent?"

Her brown eyes flashed. "What did you say?"

"They talk about you around here." An angry, mocking note seeped into my words. "I've heard all about the hotshot agent who's supposedly mastered abjuration sorcery—"

"*Supposedly?*"

"—so I can't help but wonder, if you're so goddamn smart, why are you wasting your time chasing common crooks?"

My mocking sneer came out stronger on those last words. Antagonizing her would accomplish nothing, but for some reason, I was seriously pissed off and I wanted to get *some* kind of reaction out of her.

"I am not wasting my time," she retorted furiously. "I'm keeping the world safe from scumbags and lowlifes like you!"

My blood boiled, my temper rising faster than a toddler's blood sugar in a candy store, and Lienna's glower burned with answering rage. I had the sudden violent urge to lunge across the table and—

Wait, what? I didn't hit women—in fact, I didn't usually hit men either—but brutal fury was building in my chest, making me vibrate.

Lienna's fingers twitched into fists like she was fighting the urge to magically Hulk-smash me. We were roughly three words away from an all-out brawl—which I would definitely lose, being handcuffed to a table—but I wanted a fight anyway, and that wasn't normal.

As the realization hit me, I drew in a long breath, searching for control.

"This is wrong," I began, sounding only rudely assertive instead of outright aggressive. Baby steps. "You aren't actually angry."

"Don't tell me—"

"It isn't real!" I accidentally shouted, my frustration ramping into blistering fury in an instant. I breathed deep again. "These aren't our emotions. They're—"

An ear-splitting alarm erupted through the room.

"—Quentin's," I finished, the shrill blare drowning me out.

Something hit the interrogation room door so hard the bang was audible over the alarm. Lienna leaped out of her chair. I launched up too, but chained to the table, I had nowhere to go.

Another thump, more powerful this time. The door shook. Lienna reached inside the hemp satchel she carried over her shoulder.

The door exploded and a fireball hurled toward my face.

2

YOU MIGHT THINK that when a fireball comes blazing toward your skull, your life would flash before your eyes. Mine didn't. And I was super okay with that. Now wasn't the time to relive my somber existence.

An instant before the fireball incinerated my face, Lienna's voice rang out and a bright blue barrier radiated across the room. The fiery orb of death burst against it, spraying liquid flames in every direction.

Lienna clutched a wooden Rubik's Cube, which glowed with the same blue light as the barrier that had saved my ass. And my face.

Through the mangled doorway lumbered a Dwayne-Johnson-sized Neanderthal. He had to turn sideways to fit his massive shoulders—shoulders crawling with fire—through the frame. He looked less like the Human Torch and more like fiery lava was snaking down his arms. Thick liquid dripped off his fingers and hit the floor, where it ate into the dusty linoleum.

Interesting. A fire mage? That was my best guess.

He stalked into the room, accompanied by a leaping inferno and ribbons of smoking lava. Mindless fury twisted his face.

Lienna lowered her cube, and the blue wall of safety disappeared. My first reaction was that this seemed like an inherently stupid thing to do, but before I could relay my feedback, she pulled a marble from her satchel, shouted an incantation I couldn't hear over the screaming alarm, and flung it at the intruder.

The small sphere struck the man with a dull pulse. His fiery veins shrank and went out with a pitiful sizzle, then his entire body relaxed as though someone had shot him full of horse tranquilizer. He staggered back, bumped into the wall, and slid limply to the floor. Lienna retrieved a fresh pair of cuffs from her satchel and fastened them around his wrists.

The whole thing, from exploding door to unconscious mage, had taken ten seconds, adding more weight to the wilder rumors about Lienna's mastery of abjuration. The lady was good.

Without a victory dance or even a fist pump, she picked up the marble, then pulled a set of keys from her satchel, which was beginning to seem like Mary Poppins's carpetbag. Did she have a coat rack in there too?

"I've never seen a pyromage do that before," I remarked.

"Volcanomage," Lienna corrected as she jammed a key into the lock that bound my cuffs to the table and popped it open. "Follow me."

"Hold up a sec! We're not going out there, are we?"

The prospect of rushing out into whatever acrimonious chaos was ravaging the precinct didn't thrill me. If I was right about the involvement of my former pal and fellow inmate Quentin, he was flooding the entire precinct with contagious rage that would only keep building. That's what empaths did: they made people feel all the feels. In this case, all the "incoherent fury" feels.

Meaning Vesuvius the Lava Wizard was the first of many, many magical dangers outside the interrogation room.

Lienna turned toward the door. "We are."

I waved my handcuffed wrists at her back. "Can you at least unlock me first?"

"No."

Angry heat rose from my chest and into my head, but I stuffed it back down. Quentin's emotional manipulation magnified even the slightest irritation. If it was this bad here, how ragey were all the nasty criminals in lockup?

Lienna pinched one of her necklaces, a chain with a cat's eye dangling at the end. Between bleats of the relentless alarm, she declared, "*Ori menti defendo.*"

That nonsense word was an incantation for a sorcery artifact, and in response to the trigger word, the cat's eye pendant glowed. The tension in her shoulders loosened, and as the tight lines of anger around her full lips softened, she offered me the first smile I'd seen yet. It was small and brief, but hey, it was a smile.

"Stay behind me. You'll be fine." Then she stepped out into the hallway.

To follow or not to follow, that was the question. Cowering in an unlocked room without the protection of this sorceress was far less appealing than whatever chaos awaited us, so I accompanied her out the door.

A nightmarish barrage of sounds assaulted my ears. Over the alarm, there were people screaming, footsteps pounding, metal clanging, and stuff breaking. To my right, the wide corridor ended in a set of nice, normal double doors. To my left, the hall bent around a sharp corner, beyond which was the epicenter of hell—billowing smoke, the orange glow of flames, bright flashes of magic.

Lienna strode to the left, Rubik's Cube in hand. Fighting every instinct I possessed, I crept quietly behind her. She crouched, peeked around the corner, then tucked back behind the protective wall.

"Are the soles of your shoes made of rubber?" she yelled over the alarm as she spun the Rubik's Cube, rearranging the runes that marked each square.

I looked down at the prison-issued tennis shoes I'd been handed on my arrival. "I have no idea. Why?"

A sizzling bolt of lightning leaped out of the billowing smoke and struck the fluorescent light overhead. The plastic casing shattered, raining debris on us.

"Electramage," Lienna revealed brusquely. She poked her head around the corner again. "Let's go."

"Whoa there!" I yelled like the worst cowboy of all time, desperately grabbing for her jacket. I caught the hem and yanked her back.

She shrugged me off. "What?"

"I can't go running out there like this!"

"What do you want me to do?"

My anger flared again, and I used my cuffed hands to point at her Rubik's Cube. "Share the wealth. Load me up. Magicify me!"

Another arc of lightning lit up the hallway and left a smoking hole in the wall across from us.

"At least give me something that'll protect me from Zeus!" I pointed at the cube again. "You can make different spells with that, right? It's got like forty quintillion possible combinations, so there must be one that'll make me immune to all this shit."

"Easier said than done," she snapped.

"Come on, Agent Shen. I'm defenseless here."

Jaw tight, she looked at the Rubik's Cube. "Give me a minute."

"I'm not sure we have a minute."

But she wasn't listening. She twisted and spun the cube, muttering words I could barely make out over the alarm.

"Water—where's water?" *Blrrring!* "Psychica …" *Blrrring!* "No, not elemental shiel—" *Blrrring!* "Where's … right!"

The deep whooshing sound of a flamethrower, accompanied by a painfully bright orange glow, cascaded down the hall. A Wilhelm scream pierced the cacophony.

Lienna spun the cube once more, then thunked it against my chest. The alarm drowned out half her shouted incantation, and a pale glow washed over the cube.

My swelling rage subsided. Calm swept over me—followed by a wave of *holy shit panic* as another blast of electricity assaulted the wall.

"Did it work?" she asked. "Are your emotions back to normal?"

"Uh … yeah, I think—" As her face lit up with a proud smile, disbelief scrunched my brows. "Wait, *that's* what your spell did? You made me immune to the *empath*?"

"You asked me to—"

If my hands hadn't been cuffed, I would've thrown them in the air. "What about the electricity? The hellfire? The maelstrom of death magic about to explode us into gooey mist? *That's* what I wanted immunity from!"

Her scowl returned. "Magic isn't that simple. At least you can think straight now. You should be thanking me."

Yeah, sure. I'd thank her if I made it through this without being skewered by lightning.

Rising to her full height and setting her feet, she faced the corridor from hell. "Just stick close to me."

With that, she leaped from behind the sheltering wall and sprinted into the melee. I took one step—then stopped. She was right. I *could* think straight again, and for some reason, charging after her held no appeal.

Instead, I inched to the corner and poked my head out. Two yards away, she whipped another marble artifact at a woman lit up with crackling white electricity. The electramage stumbled and fell backward, her power snuffed out—but she wasn't the only crazed mythic in the corridor.

It looked like a **WWE** cage match on supernatural steroids. A dozen bodies in various stages of giving or taking an ass whooping were tangled in a mass brawl. Some were criminals freed from their cells, while others were MPD agents and employees.

An alchemist and a diviner, whom I'd last seen in the holding cell beside mine, were very non-magically punching the ever-loving shit out of each other. Nearby, a short, wiry man was waving his arms and yowling incoherently—and a whirlwind was forming in the middle of the hall. Dust and debris sucked into the growing tornado, the roar of wind rising above the shrieking alarm.

Lienna gave her cube a twist and shouted another incantation. A wall of blue light swept outward, and the tornado died to nothing—but magic continued to flash and blast and flare and boom while mythics flailed and bellowed and bled.

She chucked a third marble at the aeromage and he pitched over backward. As she stooped to pick up the artifact, an angered-up MPD agent with a goatee kicked her in the side, sending her, her marble, and her Rubik's Cube sprawling.

I leaned farther into the hall. Was I supposed to do something here? Run into the chaos with my cuffed hands and bellow creative but totally pointless threats at Lienna's assailants?

The agent went for another kick, but Lienna rolled out of the way, sweeping his other leg out from under him, then elbowed him across the jaw when he hit the ground. She didn't just kick magical ass; she kicked literal ass too. And she looked good doing it.

Well then! It sure seemed like Agent Shen had things perfectly under control, so my services were definitely not required. I couldn't help anyway—not with her fancy-dancy anti-magic cuffs around my wrists.

I waited a few seconds more for her to reclaim her wooden spell cube before sliding back into the safe stretch of corridor. I awkwardly dusted off my jumpsuit, even more awkwardly ran a cuffed hand through my short brown hair, then strode away from the brawl.

Looking back on my life—which I'd spent, more often than not, on the proverbial wrong side of the tracks—I hadn't developed a soft spot for law enforcement. As a general rule, people who became cops, detectives, and agents were also the types who delighted in wielding their power like a goddamn sledgehammer. And I didn't enjoy taking the hits.

Not that I was fragile or anything. I wasn't a pane of glass here. More like a solid and reasonably handsome marble statue. You know, the type that would crack under a sledgehammer, but not straight-up shatter.

Anyway. The point is I don't trust cops, I don't like cops, and I'm confident those feelings are mutual. Same for MPD agents and their ilk. So, with only the mildest twinge of guilt, I waltzed toward freedom.

Okay, "waltz" isn't quite the right word. I bolted like a desperate fool. Can you blame me?

Bound wrists poised in front of me, I careened through the double doors, down another hall, and body-checked the push bar on a door conveniently marked with an exit sign *and* a staircase sign. Gotta love municipal safety regulations. Not even the mythic freakin' police could ignore them.

As I charged up the first flight of stairs, the alarm went silent. My ears rang with a phantom echo of the discord. Taking the steps two at a time, I considered that I was about to run into the streets wearing handcuffs and a gray jumpsuit. Problem for future me. Right now, present me's priority was getting the hell away from this place.

I reached the first landing and glimpsed an open door, a bland carpeted hallway beyond it.

In mid-step, my whole body lifted off the ground as though gravity had called it quits. I kicked like a drowning deep-sea diver, but it was no use. I was an untethered helium balloon in an empty stairwell.

"Where do you think you're going?"

Captain Blythe stepped into the open doorway, one hand stretched toward me. Her arm quivered from strain, but it didn't show on her face—surprising, since a telekinetic's mental strength was limited by their physical strength. My six-foot frame wasn't *that* lean, which meant Blythe was hella strong.

She jerked her arm sideways. I flew into the wall and the solid *thwack* shuddered through my bones. I slid down and landed on wobbly legs.

"Was that necessary?" I moaned.

Her fingers curled into a fist. My throat tightened, cutting off my air, and I clawed helplessly at my neck. Holy shit, she was Force-choking me! It would've been so cool if I hadn't been dying.

My lungs burned for air and my vision faded. Just when I thought I'd pass out, her hand relaxed. My throat opened and I gasped. Giving up on dignity, I slid down the wall and sat hard on the floor.

As I sucked in lungfuls of sweet, sweet air, Blythe strutted toward me. She crouched to meet my eyes, her pale blue gaze promising all kinds of regret for my rash escape attempt.

"You don't want me as your enemy, Morris," she said, barely louder than a whisper. "But you just can't help yourself, can you?"

3

WHEN I FIRST LANDED in an MPD holding cell, I'd realized immediately that a spell prevented any magical high jinks from going down within the cell block. It'd been easy to guess—even without anti-magic cuffs on, it'd felt like having a limb amputated.

Somewhere between then and my interrogation, that spell must have failed.

Gripping my elbow with painful pressure, Blythe steered me through the diminishing chaos. We passed unconscious people, bleeding people, and angry people. Everyone was angry, but it wasn't "tear out the throat of anyone nearby" rage anymore.

Avoiding provocative eye contact with anyone, I slunk beside Blythe as she passed the interrogation room and turned the corner.

Lienna, with the help of a few agents, had extinguished the battle. Various mythics were in handcuffs or magic-snuffing bracelets. Others were unconscious and/or bleeding all over the floor. Lienna was leaning over one such victim and chanting softly. Something small glowed in her hand.

"Agent Shen," Blythe called as Lienna straightened. "I want every inmate who isn't dying locked in a cell in the next five minutes."

"Yes, ma'am." Lienna hesitated as though unsure if she was about to poke a shark in the eye. "How did this happen? The holding spells—"

"—were tampered with," Blythe cut in. "Might have been an inside job. The security guild is on the way to rebuild them."

Half listening, I watched a tall, spindly dude with bright red hair down to his shoulders—the precinct's resident healer?—pour a potion on a woman's gouged arm. He had a backpack full of vials and plastic baggies, which he administered to the worst-off combatants with frazzled expediency.

Blythe slapped a hand between my shoulder blades and shoved me at Lienna. "Keep an eye on this one. I caught him halfway up the south stairwell."

Lienna glared at me. "Of course you did."

I wasn't sure what a shit-list looked like—aside from the expected scatological characteristics—but I had the distinct feeling I was officially on one.

"At least the containment floor didn't fail," Blythe grumbled as she surveyed the damage. "The moment you're done here, Agent Shen, I want you on the hunt for the empath."

On the hunt? So, Quentin had escaped. I wasn't surprised.

Quentin was many things: the most powerful empath alive, according to basically everyone; a cunning bastard who didn't hesitate to use his ample power; my former guildmate and coworker; and the nearest thing I had to a best friend. Going out for beers to shoot the shit and complain about work once or twice a week was something friends did, right?

I wasn't one hundred percent sure on that. Friendship wasn't really a thing I did.

"Containment floor?" I asked, homing in on Blythe's offhand comment. "What's that?"

The captain headed back down the hallway.

"You're going to leave me hanging like this?" I called after her.

Lienna grabbed my sleeve and hauled me to the end of the corridor, where a sorry-looking bunch of inmates in cuffs were sitting on the floor.

She plunked me down against the wall. "If you try to escape again, I will send your testicles into another dimension."

Well, that was horrifying. And intriguing. "Can you actually do that?"

"Test me and find out." With a stern stare, she hurried off to arrange my and my fellow detainees' immediate return to our cells—or so I assumed.

"Hey Kit," an unpleasantly familiar voice said. "What's up?"

Slouched against the wall across from me was the equally unpleasant face of my cellmate, Duncan. A pair of handcuffs like mine enclosed his wrists, which was a damn relief to see.

"Not much," I replied. "Just trying to survive the Mystical Melee at MagiPol."

"It got a little wild, didn't it?" he agreed casually, as though we were discussing the weather forecast. Overcast skies and a chance of prison riot.

Duncan was … well, let's just say he was a real piece of work. I've watched a lot of crime shows in my day, and I even endured a stint in juvie, but no episode of *Criminal Minds* could've prepared me for Duncan. He might have been a middle-aged white dude with a potbelly and a Jason Alexander hairline, but he scared the shit out of me.

Our first conversation, after I'd been unceremoniously tossed into a cell with him, had gone something like this.

Him: "What're you in for?"

Me: "Fraud, I guess. You?"

"Murder."

"Oh."

"Yeah."

"Just the one?"

"No."

There I'd hesitated. What was the protocol in that situation? Should I inquire further or let it go? Drunks, pickpockets, and street-corner drug dealers I could handle. Murderers, though? Then again, if I was sharing cramped quarters with a serial killer, I wanted to know how many eyes I should keep open while sleeping on the cot above his.

So I'd asked, as nonchalant as him, "How many?"

"Seventeen," he'd replied with a yawn.

Our subsequent conversations—which I'd participated in so as not to offend the nice serial killer—had revealed he was a hydromage. I'd assumed drowning would be his *modus operandi*, since he was a magical murderer who could control water, but he'd explained how he preferred to slowly suck all the moisture from his victims' bodies.

Delightful.

I resumed my observation of the demolished post-riot hallway, and a few minutes later, an MPD agent with a shaved head, lumberjack beard, and shoulders like a linebacker arrived to escort me and Duncan to our holding cell. The solid concrete walls, with a cage-style front facing a wide corridor, had sadly survived the riot with only a few scorch marks.

The agent pulled open the cell door. "Get in there."

We complied. The man swung the door shut, locked it, and marched back the way we'd come.

"Hey!" I yelled after him. "What about the cuffs?"

Duncan and I were still sporting our incarceration bracelets, which weren't particularly comfortable.

My cellmate, already perched on his cot and staring unblinkingly at the sink, seemed unbothered. A minuscule bead of water clung to the faucet for several long seconds, then lost its hold. It plinked against the drain, and a nearly imperceptible smirk slipped onto Duncan's lips.

I shuddered. If only Quentin's emotional storm had worked out as well for me as it had for him.

HANDCUFFS SUCK.

A loud clang jolted me from an uncomfortable doze. As alertness returned, so did the dull ache in my arm and shoulder joints, and the much sharper ache in my wrists where the metal bands dug into my flesh. Leaving a prisoner in handcuffs overnight should be illegal.

Stifling a groan, I sat up, almost knocking my thin blanket off my bunk.

"Kit Morris." The Paul Bunyan agent stood at the cell door. He rapped his knuckles against the metal bars. "Get over here."

I didn't move. "What's up, Lumberjack Stan?"

Seeing I would require further encouragement to get off my ass, he held up a plain manila envelope. "This is for you."

"What is it?"

He waved the envelope and waited.

I swung my legs off my bed and dropped to the floor. Duncan was sitting on the lower bunk, staring fixedly at the toilet, and we ignored each other as I ambled to the bars.

"So, what is it?" I asked again. "A love letter?"

He pushed it between the bars. "It's your summons. For sentencing. For your *crimes*," he added at my blank expression.

Oh. Crimes. Right.

I took the envelope and tore it open with my teeth—damn handcuffs. Inside was a multi-page form titled *C-1001A-34: Summons for Sentencing – Judiciary Council*. A lot of jargon that fell somewhere between legalese and bureaucratic bullshit filled the page, but the important bits explained that a panel of MPD judges would sentence me on Thursday, June 14 at 8:30 a.m.

Sentence me to what, though? Community service? Jail time? A *Braveheart*-style draw and quarter? I frowned at the page. What were they even charging me with?

Don't get me wrong. I knew I'd broken a few rules during my time at KCQ. I just didn't know *which* rules.

Flipping to the next page, I discovered an equally dense block of text that filled me in with chilling concision:

9 count(s) of Conspiracy to Commit Fraud

16 count(s) of Inflicting a Mythic Ability on a
   Non-mythic Entity

3 count(s) of Second-degree Larceny involving a
   Mythic Ability

23 count(s) of Theft over $10,000

1 count(s) of Petty Theft under $2,000

9 count(s) of Aggravated Assault with a Mythic Ability

A fun note at the end revealed the MPD could add, remove, or alter the charges at their discretion any time prior to sentencing.

So … not community service, then.

At the metallic rasp of a key sliding into a lock, I looked up. The agent swung the cell door open.

"Captain Blythe wants to see you." He gestured impatiently. "Let's go."

I folded the packet and shoved it in my jumpsuit pocket. "You're a courier *and* an escort? What a career!"

Scowling, he led me away from the cell block. Though my mind was on other things—namely my impending doom, aka sentencing hearing—I was a bit surprised. Draconian authoritarians or not, these agents sure could clean up an ugly mess real fast. It'd been less than twenty-four hours, and everything looked about the same—minus the scorch marks and broken walls. I couldn't help but imagine an agent dressed like Mickey Mouse in *Fantasia*, musically directing dancing mops around the precinct.

Grumpy the Wonder Beard chained me to the table in a new interrogation room—or I assumed it was a different room. I couldn't see any puddles of hardened lava on the floor.

Less than a minute later, Captain Blythe and Agent Shen walked in, looking as put-together and unfrazzled as they had yesterday.

"*Déjà vu*," I remarked. "I feel like we've already done this."

Blythe sat across from me. "Do you know Quentin Bianchi?"

No time for cordiality, I guess. "Yeah."

No point in evading the question. Quentin had been taken into custody weeks before me and had spilled an unknown number of beans about his guild and acquaintances. I couldn't imagine *why*, but the empath always had a reason.

"How would you describe your relationship with Quentin?" the captain asked.

I rolled my eyes thoughtfully toward the ceiling. "We were like Jay and Silent Bob—no, more like Timon and Pumbaa."

Her face went so stony that it lost all resemblance to living flesh.

"We were guildmates," I added expansively. "We worked together on a few assignments."

"What kind of assignments? How often? How closely did you work together?"

I leaned back in my chair as far as my handcuffs would allow. "Can't find him, can you?"

Blythe and Lienna stiffened, and I had to hold back a smile.

"You arrested him, what, four weeks ago? That's pretty good. Holding him that long, I mean." I tried to buff my fingernails on my sleeve, but the rattling chains ruined the effect. "And now you need my help to catch him."

"We don't *need* anything from you," Lienna retorted coolly. "But if you recall those embezzlement and extortion investigations I mentioned yesterday—and the potential new charges against you—maybe you'll consider sharing whatever information you have about Quentin."

"I'll consider it, but first I want to know what, specifically, I get out of this deal."

Blythe's eyes narrowed. "What?"

"Telling the judge how I was a good little convict who helped you catch the bad empath isn't nearly enough motivation for me to turn snitch. You're gonna have to do better than that."

Blythe assessed me with stony calculation, and I let the silence stew. There was a shift in power happening here and I fully intended to take advantage of it.

Lienna stepped away from her spot by the one-way mirror. "What do you want, Kit?"

"Two things. First, I want leniency."

Blythe raised a skeptical eyebrow. "Meaning?"

"Meaning, in exchange for helping you re-arrest Quentin, I want the assault charges against me dropped, because those are bullshit, and I want leniency in sentencing for the rest of the charges. You're important enough to make that happen, aren't you, Almighty Empress of the Precinct?"

A slight twitch dimpled Blythe's cheek, but I couldn't tell if she was amused or annoyed. "And your second request?"

"To catch Quentin, I can't just sit here and psychoanalyze his behavior patterns. Pro-tip: psychoanalyzing empaths is a waste of time." I braced my elbows on the table. "To do this properly, I need to go out there and find him."

"Hell will freeze over before I set you loose—"

"Not by myself." I rolled my eyes. "With the abjuration queen. Agent Shen can handle me, don't you think? This'll all go much smoother—and faster—if I accompany her on the manhunt. I know how Quentin operates."

"Then you can tell Agent Shen exactly that," Blythe snapped, "and your ass stays right here in the precinct."

I sighed. "Okay. I'll give you a freebie so we're on the same page. Do you know how Quentin's abilities work?"

"He's an empath," Lienna answered swiftly. "He can influence the emotions of the people around him."

"Yeah, that's the baby version. Quentin is the Thanos version of an empath." And I had it on good authority that, unlike most empaths, his gift was of super-villain quality. "His power works in two ways—input and output. The input is intuitive. He can sense the emotions of anyone nearby."

"We know th—" Blythe began irritably.

"Did you know emotions are contagious?" I interrupted. "When you see someone who's scared, you get a zing of fear too. When you see happy people, you feel uplifted—unless you're completely heartless, like a precinct captain or something."

Blythe's lips thinned.

"Now imagine how contagious emotions are when you're a powerful empath." I tapped my finger on the tabletop. "The output is where things get interesting. If Quentin makes someone feel scared, the input kicks in and he feels their fear. That kicks *his* fear up, which feeds back into his target, which feeds back into him, and the next thing you know, everyone in the room is terrified out of their mind."

"Or," Lienna muttered, "everyone around him is thrown into a murderous rage."

Pretty much exactly. By my educated guess, jail had really pissed Quentin off. And while he was having a temper tantrum over his imprisonment, the abjuration spells on the holding cells collapsed. His anger had gone off like a nuke, which bumped everyone else's rage-o-meter into the red, which fed back into his own ire. One thing led to another, and well, we all know what followed.

"And that," I concluded cheerfully, "makes Quentin extra super dangerous."

Of course, various factors affected, and limited, Quentin's ability—things like targeting a specific person or a group, how susceptible someone was to the emotion, the distance of his target, and Quentin's own mental state. But I didn't mention any of that.

"So." I propped my chin on my hands. "I know how to find Quentin and how to handle him. If you want to catch him before he skips right out of the country, you need me out there with Agent Shen."

Blythe studied me for a long minute, and though her expression remained stoic, I could see the hot frustration building in her eyes. Her quarry already had an alarming head start. She didn't have time to waste sparring with me, and she knew it.

I let a smile creep onto my face. "Did I mention I know *exactly* where Quentin went the moment he escaped?"

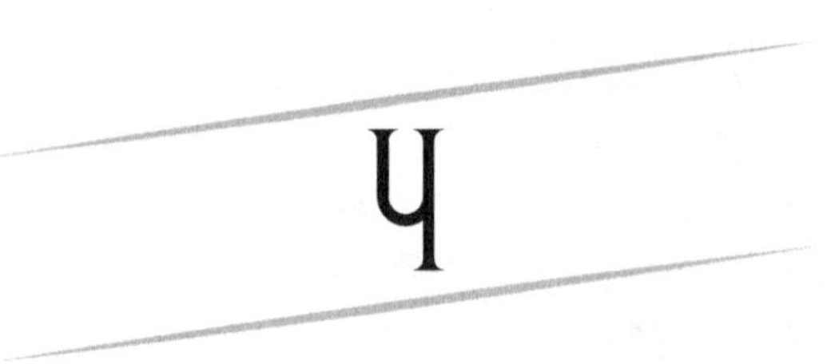

THERE ARE THREE PRIMARY REASONS I work out.

Reason one: the strength of some mythics' magical abilities is directly tied to their physical condition. The more you hit the gym, the better you can wield your power. I had no idea if I fell into that category, but neither did I have confirmation that I *didn't*, so I was on board either way. I'd upped my training regime to six days a week—cardio, weightlifting, yoga, plyometrics, swimming, aerobics, you name it. If it made your muscles burn and your lungs heave, I tried it.

After Blythe departed the interrogation room, the robustly bearded agent who'd escorted me here dropped off the street clothes I'd been wearing when I was arrested. He also handed a small fabric bundle to Lienna, then left.

Lienna pulled a key from her satchel and stepped warily toward me.

"I'm taking these off." She pointed at my handcuffs. "If you try anything remotely underhanded, I'll replace your eyeballs with pepperoni and lock you up with our K-9 unit."

I arched my eyebrows. "I have so many emotions right now. I'm excited to get these cuffs off, I'm genuinely curious about whether you can do the pepperoni thing, I'm nervous my eyeballs might be in real danger, and—"

With a deft turn of the key, Lienna popped open the handcuffs, and I broke off with a relieved sigh. Holy Sweet Baby Moses that felt good. Not just my newly freed and usable wrists, but the heady surge of confidence that came with the return of my abilities. I could feel my power, like a lightbulb had lit in my head. This wasn't the time for a test run, though—not with Lienna and her scary satchel of abjuration torture standing guard.

"And?" she prompted.

I had to think back to what I'd been saying. "And I genuinely want to know if there are K-9 puppies and whether I can meet them."

With an exaggerated eye roll, she pointed at my clothes. "Put those on. We need to keep a low profile."

Reason two: general health. I don't enjoy running out of breath halfway up a flight of stairs or struggling to carry a medium-sized grocery load home from the supermarket. Working out spares me all that unpleasantry.

Standing, I kicked off the ugly-ass tennis shoes I'd been forced to wear and paused with my fingers on the zipper of my uglier-ass jumpsuit. "You gonna turn around?"

In answer, she crossed her arms.

Fine then. I yanked the zipper down, shrugged off the sleeves, and let the whole thing fall to my ankles. Underneath, I wore boxers, a pair of socks, and nothing else.

Reason three: the subtle expression on Agent Lienna Shen's face as she watched me undress. Having worked with plenty of stomach-turning narcissists at KCQ, I do my best to avoid the realm of vanity, but it's hard not to feel good when you catch someone ogling your six-pack.

I rifled through my clothes on the table, then frowned. "Where are my boxers?"

Said boxers hadn't been washed since I'd last worn them, but anything was better than the starchy, powder-blue, flesh-abusing MPD-issue ones.

Lienna gave a small start. "Oh. Uh. We don't keep undergarments, but"—she held out the small roll of pale blue fabric—"they grabbed these for you."

Ignoring the gooseflesh rising on my skin from the chilly basement air, I took the fabric and shook it out, discovering a pair of boxers identical to the ones I was wearing. Oh, yay.

I rubbed the scratchy fabric between my finger and thumb. "Do you have any idea how itchy these things are?"

She shrugged vaguely. In fact, she didn't seem to be paying much attention to what I was saying. Her gaze kept darting around—jumping from my face to the table, then skidding from my midriff to the one-way mirror, then flicking to my left shoulder, tracing down my bicep to my forearm, and abruptly sweeping to the floor.

"So …" I said, drawing her focus back to my face. "No other undergarment options?"

"That's all we've got." Her gaze drifted down again.

"Hmm." I bounced the boxers on my palm. "So I *have* to wear these, then?"

"Yes."

I contemplated that deeply and thoroughly, then hooked my thumb in the waistband of my boxers and pushed it down an inch. Her stare jumped to my hand and her face flushed.

"Then …" I drawled as slowly as possible, dragging it out to see how many shades of pink her cheeks could achieve. "I should … finish … dressing."

She wrenched her eyes back up to my face, and when she saw my smirk, she snapped her spine straight.

"Hurry up," she barked, folding her arms again. "We're on the clock!"

"You got it."

I got both thumbs under my boxers' waistband—and her gaze dropped to her feet. Suppressing a chuckle, I stripped off my boxers and pulled on the new pair. They were as awful as their predecessors. It was like wearing a cereal box around your most personal bits.

I slid my dark wash jeans out of the pile and pulled them on. As I zipped the fly, Lienna's cautious gaze crept toward me. I flashed her a grin and she scowled back.

Pretending not to notice her attention lingering on my chest, I tugged on a white V-neck shirt, then donned a hooded, earthy green jacket, hoping my outer layers would somehow counteract the discomfort I was feeling underneath. No such luck.

Lienna selected a pendant from the collection around her neck and lifted it over her head, a shark tooth dangling from the chain. Stepping closer, she dropped it over my head.

"*Ori mens tua serenetur*," she declared.

A rune etched into the shark tooth glowed for a second, then faded away. I could still feel my powers, but the necklace had deadened them to the point of uselessness. My good mood fizzled out.

Lienna tapped her fingernail against the tooth. "Keep that on. If I see you taking it off, I'll—"

"Transform cherished body parts into deli meats or send them to a parallel universe?"

"If you're lucky. Let's get going."

"I CAN'T BELIEVE we're in a smart car."

The gate to the MPD's underground parking garage lifted and Lienna pulled the dinky vehicle out onto the street. As per the norm in Vancouver, a drizzly haze coated the pavement, leaving the streets perpetually damp. No wonder Duncan lived here. I'd been hoping, perhaps naively, that the sun would be out, but even an overcast sky was a welcome change from the windowless, subterranean prison.

Lienna turned left through a shallow puddle that threatened to submerge the eco-friendly clown car we were jammed into.

"Why don't you guys have something with more, you know, strength, power, guts?"

Stopping at a red light, she cast me an arch look. "Is your masculinity threatened by the teensy-weensy car?"

"My masculinity is threatened by this dashboard, which my knees will go right through if you hit the brakes too hard."

"We're keeping a low profile. We can't have the general public knowing that 'magic police' exist and patrol the streets. Where am I going?"

"Kitsilano area," I informed her. Had I refused to divulge a location until I was out of the precinct? Damn right I had.

The light turned, and Lienna accelerated just as a jackass truck blew through the intersection. Standard Vancouver driving. Lienna and three other drivers chastised the truck with honks, then we all went on our merry way.

"How do you expect to chase after bad guys in this thing?" I asked, picking up where we'd left off.

"I don't. A low profile and car chases are also incompatible. We're not Steve McQueen."

I gasped dramatically. "Did you just make a classic film reference? Are you flirting with me?"

She rolled her eyes. "I'm just trying to speak your language."

Not bothering with subtlety, I studied her. Was it my imagination, or was the stern Agent Shen looking more relaxed? Now that we were out of the precinct—and out from under Blythe's omnipresent shadow—the tension around her mouth had softened, and the lingering hint of pink in her cheeks from my not-quite-a-striptease brightened her complexion.

Her eyes flicked to mine, deep brown and lit by a lively, mysterious glint—until they narrowed suspiciously.

"What?" she demanded.

Diversion tactics, commence. "You're from LA, right?"

She faced the road again. "Yes."

"Why are you still in Vancouver? Don't you have a job to get back to? Criminal mythics in California to tackle to the floor?"

"I had a flight booked for tomorrow, but after the incident at the precinct, the captain requested I stay to provide support."

"Captain Blythe doesn't seem like the type to *request* things."

Lienna answered with a grunt. Did I detect a note of bitterness, mayhap?

"She's making you stay," I guessed.

"The Vancouver MPD is critically understaffed. Captain Blythe needs the help."

"Is that why she has you leading the manhunt for Quentin?"

Lienna flexed her jaw as though considering whether to answer. "I'm the most qualified agent available. I'm technically on the Rogue Response team in Los Angeles."

Technically on the team? Interesting.

"Ooh, fancy," I teased. "You must have a trophy room full of taxidermied mythic bad guys back home."

"I can't say I've ever taxidermied anyone. I'm still a rookie."

"Don't be so modest. How many rogues have you caught?"

"Including you?"

I nodded. "Yeah, sure."

She held her breath as she calculated the number in her head, then exhaled. "One."

"One?"

"Just you."

I couldn't hide my surprise. "What?"

"I transferred into the RR a week ago. Apprehending you at LAX was my first assignment."

No wonder her interrogation skills were kind of green. "Well, as your very first arrest, I can say you did a lovely job."

"Very funny."

"I'm serious. Five stars. Best incarceration service I've received so far."

All I got in response was another eye roll—but the corner of her mouth might have ticked upward. Watching her in my peripheral vision, I considered what I knew and what I'd heard. Something wasn't adding up.

"If you're only a week in and I was your first arrest," I began carefully, "where does your reputation come from? Half the precinct was buzzing about the newly arrived abjuration prodigy, and that was before you went all *Dirty Harry* during the riot."

She shrugged. Before I could try another angle of questioning, I had to direct her on where to turn. I navigated her through the neighborhood, and a few minutes later, she pulled the smart car up to the curb, cut the engine, and looked around curiously.

We were parked on a narrow road south of Kitsilano Beach. A mix of sleek, modern homes and old, behemoth multi-story residences hid behind towering maple trees. Across the street was a skinny, two-level house with a hand-painted sign that boasted, "Kitsilano Klairvoyant."

"We're here," I announced unnecessarily, then squeezed out of the car and tugged my clothes straight. Lienna joined me, her hand buried in her satchel like an Old Western Sheriff gripping his pistol as she faced the sign. Her forehead wrinkled with skepticism.

I crossed the street and walked onto the creaky front porch, Lienna following on my heels.

Quentin came here whenever he had an important decision to make. He liked mystical confirmation before entering new, risky ventures—and he liked to rule out any mystical portents of "do that and you might die." I'd come along a few times, and I kind of got the appeal.

It wasn't *that* unreasonable to assume he'd show up fresh out of jail, seeking guidance. If I was correct, it would play right into my leniency deal with Captain Blythe. And if I was wrong? Oh well. It'd gotten me out of the precinct, away from all but a single agent, and into a magic-suppressing necklace that was far easier to remove than magic-suppressing handcuffs.

Stifling a smile, I hit the doorbell, and a chime rang through the house's interior.

Visible through the frosted glass, the shadow of a tall, slender figure approached. The door opened, revealing Jansen Jenkins, the Kitsilano Klairvoyant. Technically speaking, Jenkins was a diviner—a mythic who used various tools and rituals to predict the future. Or as Jenkins put it, to "translate messages from the spirit world."

A clairvoyant was something else entirely, but he called himself one as a marketing gimmick. He was one of a very few mythics who used magic in full view of the general public without revealing the true and full nature of his abilities. It was a fine line to walk, but he walked it well.

At Jenkins's appearance, Lienna's expression shifted to surprise. Diviner stereotypes consisted of eccentric, heavily accessorized women with an affinity for colorful silk scarves, but Jenkins was in his fifties, well over six feet tall, beanpole thin, and sported a long, pointed nose and a short, conservative haircut. With his white dress shirt, neatly tucked into his black dress pants, he resembled an English butler more than a West Coast fortune teller.

He looked us both up and down with his typical reserved expression, then offered me the faintest smile. "You're Quentin's friend."

"Kit," I reminded him.

"And you are?" he asked Lienna.

She flashed me a vaguely alarmed look as though just realizing she had no idea why we were here or what our strategy was supposed to be, then plucked her badge from her satchel and held it up like a shield. "Agent Lienna Shen."

Should I have warned her that her badge and agent title would get her approximately nowhere with this guy? Probably—and yet, I had no regrets about failing to do so.

A sour look squeezed Jenkins's face. "And what business does MagiPol have here? Unless you've come for a reading?"

She dropped her badge back in her bag. "You mentioned Quentin. Do you know him well?"

"He is a regular client," Jenkins stated flatly.

She flicked another glance at me, then asked, "Have you seen him recently?"

Jenkins crossed his arms in response. "I can't be sure. However, I find my memory is much sharper after a reading. Or two."

The message was clear: to get information, we needed to pay up. Businessmen like the Kitsilano Klairvoyant didn't work for free. Lienna shifted her weight as though debating her options, then sighed.

"Do you take credit?"

5

JENKINS'S READING ROOM hid behind a purple curtain—velvet, of course—at the back of his house. Salt lamps and herb-scented candles softly lit the massive bookshelves that lined the walls. In the middle of the space was a low, circular, glass-topped table surrounded by a trio of wooden chairs.

Three chairs … almost like Jenkins had predicted he'd soon have two guests.

"Please take a seat," he murmured. As we obeyed, the diviner narrowed his eyes at me. "I did not expect you to be in league with the MPD, young man."

Lienna opened her mouth, possibly to explain how I was a subjugated prisoner coerced into aiding my captors at the risk of an eternity in solitary confinement, and I snuck her a warning look. She shut her mouth.

If we wanted answers from this guy, I needed to control what we shared with him or he would clam up like Al Capone's most loyal lackey. Not that him clamming up was all that big of a deal, but I had an act to maintain.

"Special circumstances," I replied quickly. "Quentin is in danger. I'll do anything—or work with anyone—to help him."

Jenkins frowned. "In danger? What kind of danger?"

"He escaped MPD custody yesterday—but you know that, because he came to see you."

Jenkins blinked in surprise, and I suppressed a triumphant grin. What do you know? I'd guessed right.

I leaned forward. "Did he tell you what he's after?"

"After?"

I studied his startled expression, weighing the likelihood of sincerity, and decided he was totally out to sea. Good.

"He escaped for a reason," I continued smoothly. It was entirely possible I wasn't lying. Quentin always had a plan. "And whatever he's going for next—it's gonna be nasty stuff. Plus, Quentin *wrecked* the precinct on his way out. He's this close"—I held up my finger and thumb an inch apart—"to a big fat bounty on his head."

"Once the guilds start hunting him, he won't stand a chance," Lienna added, catching on to my tactic. "But if we find him first, we can protect him—from the MPD, from a bounty, and from himself."

Worry creased Jenkins's forehead. "I see."

"What do you know about KCQ?" she asked.

"They are a psychic guild parading as a law firm—or *were*, I should say. They were disbanded, were they not? Hardly a shame. Thieves and con artists, the lot of them." He clicked his tongue. "I advised Quentin more than once that he should extract himself. It was foolish of him—and you as well, Kit—to get involved."

A little late for that advice, Judgy McJudgerson.

"The guild's fall was quite dramatic," he went on in a reminiscent tone. "A guild master murdered by another guild? The celestial spirits were in a tizzy."

Quite dramatic was a massive understatement. Around a month ago, another guild, the Crow and Hammer, had caught wind of KCQ's more creative endeavors. Quentin had ended up in MPD custody as a result—and our guild master, Rigel, had proceeded to lose his mind. He'd been obsessed with Quentin's power and blamed the interfering guild for his super-empath's arrest.

And, like a genius, he'd launched a vendetta against them.

We psychics have cool powers and all, but in direct combat, mages and sorcerers kick our asses every time. Needless to say, our GM's attack on the much grittier Crow and Hammer had been an unmitigated disaster-circus. Rigel had been killed, our new office had burned to the ground, and our guild had been disbanded. Cue my doomed flight from the city.

The whole thing was insane. You could write an entire book about that shitshow.

"You don't know the half of it, man," I told Jenkins. "Now MagiPol is trying to save face, and if Quentin causes any more trouble, they'll make an example of him whether he deserves it or not."

Ignoring my badmouthing of her precious employer, Lienna kept her focus on the diviner. "If we can get to Quentin first, we can help him escape serious charges and get his life on track."

Jenkins pondered everything we'd said, and I let him stew over it. Silence was a powerful tool if you knew how to use it.

As it stretched into uncomfortable territory, Lienna glanced at me. I gave my head a tiny shake. Just wait.

"I saw Quentin yesterday at around nine p.m.," Jenkins admitted. "He came in for a reading."

Lienna leaned forward. "Do you know where he is now?"

"I haven't the foggiest notion."

"What sort of reading did you do for him? Tea leaves? Tarot cards?"

Jenkins wrinkled his nose. "Nothing so crude. For Quentin, I typically employ a more complex methodology."

"Scrying?" she guessed.

"Bibliomancy."

I was sort of insulted. During my few visits with Jansen Jenkins, I'd qualified only for his "crude" tactics.

"Oh." She hesitated. "How does that method work?"

"Perhaps you would find a demonstration educational. You have already paid for a reading, and you may gain some useful insight for your investigation."

She opened her mouth.

"Sure," I said before she could turn him down.

She threw me a "don't you dare" glower, but Jenkins was already nodding agreeably.

"Perfect," he said. "Please select a handful of books from anywhere in the room."

I looked around. There were a shit-ton of books in here. "Does it matter how many?"

"Whatever speaks to you."

Standing, I headed for the bookshelves, Lienna's gaze following my every move.

As I pretended to contemplate the leather spines, I considered the real reason I was here. Regardless of my and

Lienna's story weaving—which had been surprisingly fun—finding Quentin was extremely low on my priority list. The dude could take care of himself. He'd made his escape and I had zero desire to see my friend locked up again.

The real reason I was out in the burbs, across the inlet from the MPD precinct, was to manufacture my own escape.

All I needed was a solid distraction where I could slip the shark-tooth artifact off my neck. My powers would return, and I could be gone in a blink. The problem, however, was what came next—I'd be on foot in a residential neighborhood I didn't know well. And Lienna and her collection of weaponry would be right behind me.

Maybe it was best to bide my time.

I returned to the table with three books: a collection of Shakespearean plays, because one of my foster parents had shipped me off to theater camp one summer and I'd returned home speaking exclusively in iambic pentameter; an illustrated edition of the *Kama Sutra*, because I wanted to see Lienna's and Jenkins's faces when I handed it over; and a leather-bound Bible, because ... did it really matter? I had my reasons.

Jenkins stood the three books upright on the table. My *Kama Sutra* selection didn't get a reaction out of the old guy, but it did elicit an extra special eye roll from Lienna.

Mission. Accomplished.

With the books precariously standing on their ends, Jenkins had us close our eyes while he stoically whispered in an ancient-sounding language. This was something he did at the beginning of all his readings to "communicate with the spirits in the ethereal world." Apparently, the spirits spoke Latin or Sanskrit or whatever.

I cracked an eye open and peeked at Lienna. Her eyes were firmly shut, her mouth twisted in a frown. Hmm. Take off the necklace now, perhaps?

Before I could decide, a book tilted over and landed with a thump. Jenkins halted his chant, and he and Lienna opened their eyes to study the big ol' Bible lying on its face, while the other two books stayed right where Jenkins had set them.

"Are you religious, Kit?" he asked in a musing tone.

"Hell no. Have you ever met a mythic who is?"

His bony shoulder lifted in a small shrug. "You might be surprised."

I waited for him to ask why a Christian Bible would hold significance for me, prepared to evade the question, but he merely pondered the book.

After a moment, he directed me to place the Bible spine down on the table, holding the front and back cover with my index fingers very gently. Then he told me to close my eyes and let go.

I did. The book flopped open. Under his instruction, I raised my right hand and placed it on an exposed page.

"Thank you," he said. "You may open your eyes now."

The diviner took the Bible and squinted at the passage that had been under my palm.

"'Who is this coming up from the wilderness like a column of smoke, perfumed with myrrh and incense made from all the spices of the merchant?'" he read. "'Look! It is Solomon's carriage, escorted by sixty warriors, the noblest of Israel, all of them wearing the sword, all experienced in battle, each with his sword at his side, prepared for the terrors of the night.'"

He looked from me to Lienna and back, possibly hoping for some amazed *oohs* and *aahs*. Neither of us reacted.

Closing the book, he gently set it down. "King Solomon of the Israelites denotes wisdom, and this particular text presents him as a powerful warrior with an army of experienced allies. The spirits suggest you will need assistance from those who are wiser and more experienced than you."

Lienna pressed her lips together. "Can the spirits be … more specific?"

"Conflict is in your future. I am sensing a battle, as the text states. A dangerous fight during which you will need allies by your side."

"Sixty of them?" I asked.

"The specific number is irrelevant. I should note the obvious romantic implication, as well. This passage is from the Song of Solomon, also known as the Song of Songs. It is a love poem. A highly erotic one at that."

Mouth slightly agape, I glanced at Lienna, who caught me looking and replied with a dark glare.

"What about the smoke?" she asked Jenkins. "And the spices?"

"That is an interesting component. Quentin's reading also involved smoke. The selected text was from a Rudyard Kipling poem. I believe the line was, 'A woman is only a woman, but a good cigar is a smoke.' There was more, though I can't recall it. I do not waste my recreational time reading colonial poetry."

I drummed my fingers thoughtfully on the table. This whole "investigation" was just a means to an end, but I couldn't help feeling intrigued. "What do you think his text meant? What was your interpretation?"

"A woman will play an integral role in his future, although not as integral as the metaphorical cigar and its smoke." Jenkins gave a modest shrug. "I am uncertain about the significance of the smoke, but its mention seemed to please Quentin."

I was sure it had.

Lienna shifted in her chair. "Is there anything else you can tell us about Quentin's reading?"

"Those were the significant particulars."

With a quick glance to see if I was planning to say anything useful, she rose to her feet. "Well, I appreciate your help."

The diviner raised his skeletal frame from his chair and issued her a sardonic smile. "Anything for the MPD."

The three of us single-filed down the hallway toward the front door, with Lienna leading the exodus and Jenkins bringing up the rear. Midway through our journey, I felt the old man's hand slip into my back pocket, which was startling for all the wrong reasons.

I flung a "what in the gropey hell was that, you old creep" look over my shoulder, but his expression was solemn and he placed a shushing finger over his lips.

That didn't make me feel better.

I put my hand in my back pocket and felt a small piece of paper. He hadn't copped a feel; he'd slipped me a note.

As I bent down at the front door to tie my shoes, I stealthily pulled the note from my pocket, eyeing it as I fumbled with my laces. It was his slick, professionally designed business card: "The Kitsilano Klairvoyant. Vancouver's Premiere Psychic Services." But the phone number printed on the card was crossed out and he'd scratched another one above it.

I flipped the card over and found a handwritten message that made my eyes pop. It simply read, "For when you escape."

6

WHEN I ESCAPED. Not *if*.

Lienna hadn't revealed I was a prisoner, but the old diviner seemed to have, well, *divined* that nonetheless. And he also knew I didn't plan on staying one.

But what was the phone number? A hotline for fugitives on the run from the MPD? Because that would have been super helpful a few days ago when I was attempting to cross international borders.

As Lienna led me down the Kitsilano Klairvoyant's front steps, I considered our surroundings. My abjuration chaperone had her back to me and there was probably an alley nearby I could slip into. I wasn't wearing running shoes, but at least they had laces, so …

No. Not yet. We were a long way from catching up to Quentin, which meant I'd have plenty of opportunities— hopefully better ones—to escape.

Back in the smart car, Lienna started up the puny engine. "Well, that was informative."

"I'd say so," I replied, pretending not to notice the sarcasm dripping from her words. "We know to keep an eye out for smoke, and we should ask some old and wise folks for help at some point."

Scoffing, she found a gap in the intermittent residential traffic and pulled into the lane.

"You don't believe him?" I asked. "For a fancy abjuration sorceress, you're sounding a lot like a skeptic."

"I'm not skeptical of *magic*." She accelerated through a yellow light. "I'm skeptical of a man who calls himself a clairvoyant when he's actually a diviner, cheats unknowing humans out of their money, and has no reason to perform a real reading or give us truthful answers."

A white box van behind us burned through the intersection as well, garnering honks from the other cars. Vancouver traffic has no chill.

"Who says he's cheating the humans who come to him for readings?" I studied her profile. "Do you have any basis for your assumption that he's a conman?"

"His association with you and Quentin."

A scowl pulled at my lips, but I banished it. "Didn't you hear him say he disliked KCQ all along? Not *all* mythics are bad, you know."

"Says the guy with sixty-one pending charges."

"I don't even know what half of those charges are for. I was just doing my job."

"You knew what your guild was doing wasn't legal."

"You say that like I was one of the masterminds in Rigel's boardroom. I was an intern. Need to know basis and all. I was just the guy who did the thing."

"What thing?"

"With my abilities." I waved my hand vaguely. "The … whatever it's called."

Her attention darted from the road to me and back. "You don't know the name of your abilities?"

"I have it on good authority that I'm a type of psychic, but that's it." I stared through the windshield, not interested in her searching looks. "KCQ was the first time I met other mythics—and learned what a mythic was. They sure as hell weren't explaining the nuances of MPD law."

Lienna brought the car to a halt at a red light. I automatically braced as that van stopped close behind us, its grill filling the rearview mirror.

"The charges against you," she said abruptly. "A lot of them are too flimsy to hold up in front of the Judiciary Council. They hit you with a whole bunch off the top to scare you."

Was she serious? Her lips were pressed thin with displeasure, but whether over my criminal activity or the bogus stack of charges, I wasn't sure.

Her eyes turned briefly to me, a flicker of sympathy in their warm brown depths.

"Well, the scare tactic worked," I admitted quietly. "I've got two weeks until my sentencing and no lawyer to help me figure it all out."

"You don't need a lawyer."

A cop telling a suspect they didn't need a lawyer seemed like awfully shitty counsel. She might claim—or even believe—most of the charges against me would fall through, but that wasn't a risk I planned to take.

It was late afternoon, which meant rush hour was upon us and the city's traffic was becoming inevitably cluttered. As we rounded a corner, the smart car nearly rear-ended a jet-black Tesla at the tail of a long line of stationary vehicles, all waiting for a red light somewhere down the block.

Lienna hit the brakes, and the white box van, still close behind, almost turned us into an accordion, stopping a few precious inches short of our car.

"Our criminal system works differently," she continued, oblivious to our near-smoosh experience. "KCQ's lawyers were scamming the human courts. In mythic law, your sentencing is entirely up to whoever's in charge."

"Like Captain Blythe?"

"In minor cases, she makes all the decisions, but when it comes to more serious cases—"

"—like mine—"

"—you're at the mercy of the Judiciary Council. Although the captain has a big say in the matter."

The line of cars inched forward and Lienna hit her left turn signal, sliding toward the lane that would take us onto the Burrard Bridge. The white box van followed us into the lane.

"So what you're saying is that I need to turn up the charm while around Blythe and desperately hope she puts in a good word for me."

"I think the captain might be immune to all forms of charm."

"Oh, I don't know about that." I gave Lienna an exaggerated grin. "I can be *extremely* charming when necessary."

She coughed in a way that sounded a lot like a laugh. "Is that your secret psychic ability? You're a mythical charmer?"

"Is it working?"

A snicker actually escaped her. She cleared her throat and said in a bad attempt at a stern tone, "Don't forget I'm an abjuration sorcerer. I'm impervious to your powers."

Stifling another grin, I took a quick look over my shoulder. The big-ass van was still on our tail. I could see two figures inside but couldn't make out any details.

I turned back around. "Hey, have you noticed—"

"Yeah." She glanced in the rearview mirror. "Since we left the diviner's house."

"Do you think it's following us?"

"Let's find out."

As soon as we reached the far side of the bridge, she cranked the wheel to the right, screaming across two lanes of traffic and turning onto Pacific Street, completely neglecting her turn signal.

Holding on for dear life, I resisted the urge to step on an imaginary brake pedal. "Give me some warning next time you *Tokyo Drift* around a corner there, hotshot."

"I'm not Japanese." She did a speedy shoulder check, then changed lanes to pass a vehicle that was impeding her Formula 1 progress away from the van. "I'm Chinese."

"I figured that, but you are both fast and furious."

In my mirror, I saw the white box van cutting off an expensive BMW to keep up with our impromptu route change.

She took a sharp left turn under the Granville Street Bridge. "They're definitely following us."

"Who the hell are they?"

"Do any of your enemies drive an ugly white van?"

"What makes you think I have enemies?"

She whipped around another corner so suddenly my head almost bounced off the passenger side window. "You're a KCQ member."

"I *was*," I corrected.

Skyscrapers rose up around us as the smart car zigzagged toward the center of downtown, the van keeping up with us every tire squeal of the way. It struck me that this was my first genuine car chase, but the thrill was seriously dampened by two unfortunate facts: first, I wasn't driving, and second, we were in the least cool car possible.

"KCQ had a lot of enemies," she added.

I was about to retort with something about being guilty by association when she directed our runt rocket onto an off-ramp that dropped underground and into a loading bay for an upper-class hotel.

"Shit," I muttered as we bounced over a speed bump. "Dead end."

"Exactly."

She reefed on the wheel one final time, spinning the smart car a hundred and eighty degrees. We came to a stop facing the way we'd come in, surrounded by the U-shaped concrete risers of the loading bay, with the metal door behind us. Even inside the car, the place smelled like rust and trash.

"You sure about this?" I asked.

"Better here than out in public," she answered, ever the safety-conscious agent.

The van barreled down the ramp and skidded to a halt at the bottom, blocking any traffic from coming in. Or going out. We were trapped.

"I'm not an expert," I said, "but isn't this the part in the MPD manual where you call for backup?"

She pulled her phone out of her satchel and checked the screen. "No reception."

Oh goody. We were stuck two stories underground inside a concrete and steel chamber with no reception. Hopefully the kind folks inside the van were lost tourists aggressively looking for directions.

Lienna touched her cat's eye necklace, whispered the incantation, then stepped out of the car.

I hesitated. Would I be safer in the car? Or out in the open with the supercharged sorcerer? I pushed the car door open and joined her, waiting thirty feet from the van. Safety in numbers, right?

The van doors flew open and two guys in their thirties got out, both dressed like they were on their way to a performance of *The Newsies*, clad in vests, collared shirts with the sleeves rolled up, and newsboy caps. They fumed with the kind of hostility you'd expect from road-raging assholes.

A groan escaped my throat. Definitely not tourists.

Lienna side-eyed me. "You know them?"

One of the 1900s paperboys glared at me. "Kit Morris!"

I guess that answered her question.

"KCQ goons," I informed her. "Telekinetics. Jeff and Geoff."

"What?" She already had her Rubik's Cube out and was spinning the pieces around.

"Jeff with a J and Geoff with a G."

She wrinkled her nose as though the very thought of a Jeff and a Geoff residing in the same space was an abomination. "Are they brothers or something?"

"Only in spirit."

Jeff and Geoff had been up-and-comers in the law firm, but not because they were lawyers or accountants or anything that required brain cells. They had an official title involving the word "consultant," but in reality, they were muscle. Muscle without principles. The guys my boss had sent after the enemies Lienna had alluded to earlier.

"Quentin told us you got picked up," Jeff said as he retrieved three throwing knives from his vest pocket and floated them above his upturned hand. "But he didn't tell us you'd flipped."

"*Ori te formo cupolam*," Lienna uttered, and the same watery blue shield that had saved my face from the volcanomage's fireball appeared, this time in the shape of a dome that fully enclosed us.

Jeff launched a knife. The weapon noiselessly struck the magical barricade, causing the tiniest ripple, and dropped harmlessly to the ground. If it had penetrated the shield, it would have found a lovely resting place deep in Lienna's throat.

"Put down your weapons," she commanded in her most authoritative voice, "or I'll be forced to take lethal action."

"You a copper now, Kitty Cat?" Geoff growled, utilizing the closest approximation of a clever nickname he'd ever come up with.

He pulled out his own telekinetic weapons: a pair of spiky, gold-plated spheres the size of croquet balls attached together by a leather strap. I'd told him more than once that they looked like King Midas's testicles, and he usually responded by punching me in the arm or something witty like that.

"I'll make you a deal, Kitty Cat," the bearer of balls growled. "You help us kill the MagiPol bitch and we'll keep you safe."

Bristling, Lienna eyed me. I hadn't missed her palming a couple of her stun marbles in her free hand.

Not wanting her to use those on me, I said, "Counteroffer: you travel back to 1992 and return Christian Bale's wardrobe, and I'll persuade Agent Shen not to transform your intestines into vipers that will eat you from the inside out."

Jeff and Geoff looked temporarily horrified by the thought, then hurled their weapons at the shield. They ricocheted off, the ripples across the blue dome more pronounced. Lienna retaliated by chucking her stun marbles at them. They passed right through the barrier, but the telekinetics easily waved them away with their psychic power—though the effort almost caused Geoff to drop his Golden Globes.

She scowled as the paperboy mafia bombarded her shield again. *Was it just me or were the ripples getting bigger?* There was no way they were hitting it harder. These guys were slightly above average telekinetics at best; they didn't have that "dig deep" quality. That could only mean …

"This shield only lasts a couple of minutes," she whispered.

"Then do something!" I hissed back. "Can't you shoot them or liquefy their skin or whatever?"

The KCQ goons regrouped their weapons and slammed them once more against the barrier. The ripples were definitely getting bigger.

Another slam. Bigger ripples.

"MPD agents don't carry guns and the only other artifacts I have are … not ideal." She showed me another pair of stun marbles, which had already proven to be less than useful. "These are all I've got."

While Geoff continued his telekinetic barrage, Jeff focused on a manhole cover near the van's front end, wiggling it free with his mind.

"Can't the cube do anything else?" I asked.

"Not while the shield's up."

Geoff noticed his partner struggling with the massive metal disc and added his psychic power to the effort. Between the two of them, the manhole cover easily lifted into the air.

Taking advantage of their joint effort, Lienna threw another marble at Geoff, but he redirected it away.

"Last chance, Kitty Cat," Geoff warned as they edged the cover closer to the shield. "You can either join Blue Smoke or I can kick your ass."

Lienna stiffened. "Blue Sm—"

"*We* can kick his ass," Jeff sneered, not noticing her reaction.

Shooting glares at each other, the telekinetics heaved the manhole cover at the shield and the entire dome wobbled. The cover hit the concrete with a deafening crash, but Jeff and Geoff had it off the ground again in a second.

"How long does the shield have?" I asked her sharply.

"Twenty seconds. Maybe less—"

The telekinetics lobbed the cover again. It slammed against the dome and the whole thing rippled like glass about to shatter. If the shield died and they had that beast in the air, they'd render Lienna two-dimensional in a blink.

Crap.

"Remember, I'm not the bad guy here," I told her.

"Huh?"

"And don't let them squish you," I added as Jeff and Geoff picked up the cover again. It rose fifteen feet and aligned to drop on our heads.

She squinted at me. "Wha—"

The manhole cover crashed onto the dome, and as the watery wall burst apart, I shoved her hard. She stumbled backward, and the plunging cover smashed down where she'd been standing.

I tore the shark tooth necklace over my head and my powers rushed back. Damn, that felt good.

Lienna darted away, and as Geoff and Jeff co-aimed the cover at her—a more difficult feat against a moving target—I focused on the two men. Or rather, on their minds.

They hurled the cover, missing Lienna by two feet. As it hit the asphalt with an ear-splitting clang, Jeff's knives rose into the air and Geoff's golden balls floated upward with a wave of his fingers. They'd abandoned the heavy metal disc for their usual weapons—which meant Lienna had about three seconds to live.

But I was already in motion, striding toward Geoff. I swept right past his spinning orbs, walked up to him, drew my fist back, and sucker-punched him in the gut. As he doubled over, I grabbed the back of his head and slammed his face down into my knee. His nose crunched, and he ragdolled against the concrete.

Jeff gawked as his buddy collapsed, then blinked at me in disbelieving shock. I knew the moment he realized what I'd done. Rage twisted his face, and his knives spun to point at me.

He was so busy preparing to murder me that he didn't notice Lienna speeding toward him. Her fist struck his jaw so hard I heard the *crack*, and he was down before he knew what'd hit him.

Victory! With the telekinetics vanquished, I glanced around for any other dangers we might need to worry about. My peripheral vision caught a glimpse of movement, and as I started to turn back toward Lienna, sharp pain burst across my ribs.

All the muscles in my body contracted, and the world went black.

A DISCORDANT BUZZING woke me up. It sounded like a thousand seagulls with laryngitis whisper-squawking over an overturned truck hauling fresh bread.

Oddly specific, I know, but I was only semiconscious. And hungry.

My head cleared and I realized the noise wasn't seagulls but half a dozen MPD agents milling about the cargo bay in which Lienna and I had done battle with Jeff and Geoff. I was propped against the side of the smart car, and the shark tooth necklace had mysteriously found its way back around my neck. Across the loading bay, I could see that the white box van had disappeared.

Lienna stood a few feet away, scribbling on a clipboard.

I moaned and sat upright. "What the shit happened?"

She looked up from her paperwork. "Oh, you're awake."

"Did you hit me with one of those evil little marbles?"

"I had to make sure you didn't escape." She glanced around at the other MPD agents, none of whom were paying attention to anything but their own tasks, then stepped closer to me. "What did you do, Kit?"

"I was saving you, not escaping," I complained, rubbing my eyes. "I can't believe you zapped me."

She crouched to get on my eye level. "What did you do to Jeff?"

"Nothing. You're the one who punched him in the head."

"The other Geoff. You walked right up to him, and he didn't even *try* to stop you."

I shrugged. "He wasn't the sharpest spike-ball *nunchaku* in the toolshed."

She analyzed me like a specimen under a microscope. "I know you're a Psychica mythic, but mentalism usually requires touch or close proximity. Are you—"

"Where are we off to next?" I interrupted with chipper enthusiasm, fully prepared to derail this "what kind of psychic powers do you have?" guessing game. For obvious reasons, the less she knew about my magic, the better. And aside from that … let's just say most people didn't react well when they found out what I could do.

A magician—or a convict in MPD custody—never revealed his tricks, after all.

With one more sweeping assessment, she stepped away from the car. "*We* aren't off anywhere. I have suspects to interrogate, and you're heading back to the precinct."

As she signaled for an MPD cohort to come over, I scrambled to my feet.

"Hey now," I protested, trying not to sound frantic as all my plans for escape crashed and burned around me. "That wasn't the deal."

The lumberjack agent who'd escorted me to and from my cell a handful of times since my arrest walked over to us. "What do you need?"

"Jack, can you take Kit back to holding?" She nodded my way.

I couldn't help it: a grin cracked my mouth open. "Your name is *Jack?*"

The mountain man frowned. "Agent Cutter to you."

"Your name is *Jack Cutter?*" No way! This broad-shouldered, bushy-bearded, callus-handed agent was one plaid shirt and an axe away from landing himself on the cover of *Wood Cutter Weekly.* "It's a little on the nose, don't you think?"

"Keep an eye on him," she warned her co-worker. "Make sure he doesn't take off that necklace."

The tree chopper grabbed me by the crook of my elbow to lead me away, but I shook him off and turned back to Lienna. "You know they won't talk to you, right?"

"Jeff and Geoff?" she said. "Maybe not at first, but we have ways to get answers out of them."

"Not if they don't know anything."

"They know something." She returned her attention to her paperwork as Agent Cutter took hold of my arm again. Not letting me wiggle free this time, he dragged me away.

I waited until we'd traversed a good fifteen feet before I called, "That's not how Blue Smoke works."

Her head snapped up. "What?"

"You heard them. They're part of Blue Smoke."

"And what is Blue Smoke?"

I gave her a half-cocked smile. "You have no idea, do you?"

She opened her mouth, then snapped it closed and gestured angrily for Agent Cutter to bring me back over to her.

"IT LOOKS LIKE Godzilla went through here."

Lienna and I stood in the drizzling rain outside a temporary chain-link fence encircling an office building that had belonged to my former guild. The last time I'd visited, renovations had been underway on the dingy two-story structure, replacing the broken windows and scrubbing away its distinct "crack house" vibe. It hadn't been much to look at, but it'd been more than … this.

"Not Godzilla," she murmured. "A pyromage."

"A strong one."

"In a very flammable structure, yes."

The basic shape of the building remained, but all the windows were gone, sections of the roof had caved in, and scorch marks stained its walls. It was a charred mess.

I grabbed hold of the chain-link fence, and it wobbled alarmingly as I pulled myself over it in one quick movement. For a brief second, I was separated from my overseer by a six-foot fence, and the ever-present thought of escape leaped to the forefront of my brain.

But she smoothly vaulted the fence and landed beside me before I could formulate a plan beyond "run really fast." She peered into the darkened doorway of the burnt structure.

"Blue Smoke," she muttered. "A clandestine organization inside a rogue guild."

It was better than that: a clandestine organization inside a rogue guild that was masquerading as a legal guild that was posing as a respectable corporate law office that was actually neck-deep in illegal schemes, fraud, embezzlement, and blackmail. It was secret-ception.

Speaking of secrets, yes, I'd decided to play one of my aces to avoid a trip straight back into Duncan's thirsty company. Revealing what I knew about Blue Smoke—and that Quentin had been involved—was a risk, but one I was willing to take.

Lienna gave me a skeptical look. "And the Blue Smoke group met here?"

"That's what Quentin told me."

He wasn't *supposed* to tell me anything, but Quentin's lips tended to loosen after a few margaritas or daiquiris or martinis or whatever his drink of choice was on a given night. According to the empath, KCQ's late guild master, Rigel, had collected a covert group of his favorite mythics for a mysterious purpose, which none of them were fully privy to.

Quentin hadn't even known why the group was called Blue Smoke. I'd speculated that it had something to do with the made-for-TV movie starring Scott Bakula of the same name. Quentin hadn't agreed.

Of course, I hadn't let on to Lienna that I didn't know much about the group or their plans. Revealing that little reality wouldn't help me any.

The moment we stepped inside the office building, darkness swept over us. She dug into her satchel, pulled out her phone, and activated its flashlight mode. With the bright beam guiding our way, we moved carefully through the debris.

"Where is it?" she asked, stepping over a burnt two-by-four.

I scanned the overcooked wreckage. Most of the drywall that had divided the rooms was ash, which made it difficult to get oriented. About halfway down the northernmost wall, I spotted a metal pillar, about three feet wide, that stretched up to the second story. The wooden planks that had formed a closet-sized enclosure around it were little more than charcoal now.

I nodded toward the structure. "This way."

We picked a path through the maze of melted plastic, scorched furniture, and the odd lump of super-seared god-knows-what. I stopped at the pillar.

She shone her light over it. "It doesn't look like anything."

"That's the idea."

As I ran my hand over the blackened steel, searching for the indent Quentin had described, a new beam of light swept across the room. I spun around, Lienna mimicking me.

A silhouette in the doorway pointed a much brighter flashlight at our faces, and I scrunched my eyes painfully.

"This building's off-limits," the man called.

"Crap," Lienna muttered.

"Rogue mythic?" I guessed, shielding my eyes with one hand.

She released her satchel. "Security."

The man lowered his eye-abusing light enough that I could make out his clothes—a security guard uniform. As he strode into the rubble with a self-important bent to his shoulders, I eyed him. Late twenties but sporting a thick, immaculately groomed brown mustache that belonged on a much older man.

"You two can't be in here." His jaw smacked as he chewed a massive wad of pink bubblegum. "Door is that way. Move along."

"MPD." Lienna flashed her badge at him. "We're here on official business."

"Whoa there, miss. Let me get a closer look at that badge."

Rolling her eyes, she held out her badge once more.

I stifled a grin. It was nice to see someone else on the receiving end of that eye roll. It gave me a warm, fuzzy feeling.

The guard examined her badge. "I've never seen one like this before. MPD? What are you two kids trying to pull?"

Kids? Seriously, dude? He wasn't that much older than us. Big brother older, sure, but definitely not father-figure older, which was how he was acting. What did this guy do for fun? Shake his cane at teenagers, take early walks in the mall, and compare prune juice brands?

Lienna pushed her ponytail of dark hair off her shoulder. "You don't know what the MPD is?"

"No, and I'm not playing your game. Now take yourselves to the door, please."

Blinking, she glanced at me as though asking what to do. I shrugged in answer. Guess an overzealous security guard hadn't come up in her one whole case before this, which had been arresting me in LA.

Drawing herself up, she levelled the man with her stern agent stare. "I'm afraid I don't have time to explain. You'll need to contact your superiors for an explanation."

His patronizing smile fizzled away. "Excuse me?"

"Call your superiors and tell them that an MPD agent is investigating this building."

The guard crossed his arms. "I don't appreciate being the butt of practical jokes."

Of course you don't, grandpa.

Lienna mirrored his stance with a scowl. I could practically see her patience level plunging into negative numbers.

"Make the call," she ordered.

After an unexpectedly protracted standoff, during which I had to stifle several amused snorts, the guard gave in and pulled out his cell phone. He grudgingly dialed a number.

"Hey, this is Trevor Eggert." He turned half away from us as though that would prevent us from overhearing his every word. "I'm over here at the Skyler building on Clark and Powell … No … no, the one that burned down last week … Yeah …"

While Eggert tried to convey his location to whoever was on the other line, I leaned toward Lienna and whispered, "You should've just hit him with a doom marble."

Eggert finished describing the two "kids" trying to bypass his authority, then paused to listen. "Are you sure? Absolutely sure?"

Apparently, the person on the other end was *for sure* sure, because our friendly neighborhood watchman hung up with a defeated frown.

"I don't know who you two are," he grumbled, "but I'll be just outside here, so no funny business."

"Sure thing, Eggsy." I waved as he trudged back across the room, then canted my head at Lienna. "You MPD agents are like the FBI. You just say the word and all lowlier forms of law enforcement get lost, huh?"

"The system wouldn't work if MPD agents were getting arrested left and right." She gestured at the pillar. "Go ahead."

Eyebrows arched, I turned back to the steel structure. Maybe I was biased, but the MPD had too much power. Magic was a big secret, but like most good secrets, all the important people in the world were in on it—the uppermost ranks of police, military, government, and business included. And the MPD used those connections to keep mythics out of prison and law enforcement well away from magic.

Musing about checks and balances and magical oligarchies—not that I'm an expert, but you learn things when you hang out with smooth criminal types—I stepped close to the pillar again.

"What are you looking for?" she asked.

I slid my hands over the scorched surface until my fingertips bumped across a shallow etching. "This."

She felt the spot and frowned. "A rune?"

"I just need to remember the password."

"You mean the incantation?"

"Sure, yeah. An *open sesame* kind of thing."

Her eyes narrowed. "We came all this way and you don't remember the spell?"

"One of the words started with an A, I think."

"If this is all a misguided attempt to waste my time or figure out how to escape, I will make sure they tack extra years onto your sentence."

"Hold on, Kojak," I said. "How good's your Latin?"

"Very."

"Really?"

"I'm a sorcerer. I've been studying Latin since I was six."

"Okay, so can you say the word 'open' in Latin?"

"*Patentibus.*"

"… and then the word 'door'?"

"*Ianua.*"

We both waited for the glowing outline of a door to appear, Mines of Moria style. At least, that's what *I* was waiting for.

When nothing happened, I tapped my chin. "How about the Latin word for 'friend'?"

She glared at me.

"I thought it would work," I protested innocently. "I Google-translated the phrase after Quentin told me so I wouldn't forget. I'm pretty sure it was just 'open door.'"

"Latin is too complicated for an online translation. There are close to eighty versions of the word 'open,' depending on the meaning." She put her hand on the rune again and whispered, "*Ori aperio ianuam.*"

The rune beneath her fingers lit up like a glow stick and we stepped back. The bright light spun in concentric circles, and as it died down, a loud *click* echoed through the space.

Not quite believing that helpful click noise, I pushed on the pillar. Its front face swung inward like an obedient steel door, a dim red light emanating from the space behind it.

"Yeah!" I cheered. "That was easy."

She eyed the opening warily. "Too easy."

I stepped into the crimson-lit innards of the pillar and discovered a narrow staircase leading downward. "Did you expect something fancier? KCQ was a Psychica guild. Spells and shit weren't our forte. We were more into—"

"—illegal moneymaking schemes?"

Aw, how cute. She was finishing my sentences. "Rigel called them *innovative business ventures.*"

She followed on my heels as I headed down the stairs. There were more than I expected, descending closer to two stories than one. At the bottom was a small landing and a door with a normal knob. I swung it open.

The room on the other side was an exquisitely furnished concrete cube about the size of a two-car garage and bathed in the same red glow. A semi-circular wooden desk, with a sloppy pile of folders and books strewn across it, sat at the far end. One wall was lined with shelves and cabinets, and in the nearest corner, a pair of leather sofas lounged across from each other with a low coffee table between them.

I peered at the monochromatic paintings of a human brain above the sofas, then down at the floor, which featured a lovely and rather eerie etching of a Celtic knot with a twist of smoke rising through it. Seemed Rigel had prioritized his swanky hideaway over the rest of the building's renovations.

Lienna surveyed the space. "This is where Blue Smoke held their secret meetings?"

"That's what Quentin said."

"So, what're we looking for?"

"You're the detective." I shrugged. "I'm betting Quentin's already been here. Not only because the Jeffs mentioned it, but Jenkins's reading for Quentin was about smoke too."

"Did you know all along that the 'smoke' in the readings referred to Blue Smoke?"

"Never crossed my mind," I claimed guilelessly.

She swept past me and into the middle of the room, where she assessed every detail as though expecting Rigel's angry ghost to jump out from behind the cabinets.

"I assume Geoff and Jeff's job was to prevent anyone from following Quentin from Jenkins's place to this office," I added, ambling over to the desk to study a crystal decanter with a big yellow daisy as a stopper. "And considering Rigel's stick-up-the-ass tidiness, my guess is that Quentin made this mess too."

"Don't touch anything," Lienna warned as I reached for the decanter.

"Why not? Afraid I'll sully the scene with my criminal fingerprints?"

"Did Rigel always light his rooms with red?"

"No, but it suits the super-secretive mood of his underground lair, don't you think? He had a flair for the dramatic."

Frowning skeptically, she moved toward the cabinets. As she craned her neck, examining the doors and handles, I drifted back toward the center of the room. The open door beckoned.

This location, unlike Jenkins's suburb, was far more suited to escape. I could flee east into the industrial complexes, or bolt west and disappear among the destitute and homeless population of the Eastside. Plenty of highly viable options within sprinting distance.

All I needed was for Lienna to get nice and distracted by a juicy piece of evidence.

Completing her study of the cabinets, she gingerly grasped the stainless steel handle, her spine rigid. When nothing happened, she relaxed her stance and pulled the door open.

I gave her back one of my almost-as-impressive eye rolls. *I* wasn't allowed to touch anything, but she could—

The red light permeating the room vanished and a deep yellow glow ignited, faint and shimmering strangely. It emanated from the floor near the walls, and I angled my head to peer past the sofas.

A faintly glowing, butter-colored liquid the consistency of melted ice cream ran along the floor as though someone had spilled their lemonade. It spread quickly, creeping away from the wall. I stepped backward, then turned for the door. An equally glowing and creepy puddle flooded the floor in front of the only escape.

I didn't know where the liquid was coming from, but whatever it was, there was no way it wasn't a *really* bad thing.

"WE SHOULD GET OUT OF HERE," I suggested, containing the urge to shout it instead. My escape plans would have to wait. No way would Lienna not notice me bolting for freedom right now—plus, the way to freedom was blocked by a disturbing glowy puddle.

Rushing to my side, she scanned the spreading liquid. Two feet out from the walls and creeping toward us, it'd formed a mini lake across our path, too far to jump safely.

"Got a pen?" I asked her.

With a nervous frown at the fluid, she plucked a ballpoint pen from her satchel and passed it to me.

I tossed it into the liquid. It hit with a goopy splash—and acrid black smoke poofed upward as the plastic dissolved into a blue stain. One moment, it'd been a pen. Three seconds later, it was melted to nothing.

But that wasn't all. With the impact of the pen, a ripple had run through the liquid—and it changed. The consistency went from gooey, sticky, slow-moving melted ice cream to the viscosity of water.

And water moves a lot faster.

I yelped in alarm as the liquid rushed toward my feet. Lienna and I collided, then scrambled backward—but the yellow substance was rushing in from all directions. Whirling, I jumped onto the coffee table. She leaped up after me, her foot landing on a glossy magazine. It slid out from under her and she pitched backward.

I caught her flailing arm and yanked her upright. She flew forward and smacked into my chest. Clutching my shirt, she looked down. So did I.

The liquid—an alchemic potion of the flesh-melting variety, by my best guess—had scarcely covered the floor just moments ago. Now it was several inches deep.

And the level was rising.

"Shit!" I hissed. "Got anything in your magic bag of tricks for this?"

She looked up at me, and my relative cool threatened to break at the fear in her face. That alone was my answer: no, her abjuration sorcery was no help here.

I spun again, still holding Lienna's upper arms so she wouldn't topple off the table. The potion had climbed halfway up the table legs, and though it had dissolved the pen in seconds, it had no effect on the furniture. Were the objects that belonged in the room immune to its corrosive properties? Rigel wouldn't want his precious desk and documents eaten away—but I knew better than to assume the potion would spare our flesh.

My gaze scoured the room. Six feet of liquid between us and the door.

Guiding Lienna to the table's other end, I released her and pushed on the sofa's arm. If I could move it closer to the door, we could use it as a bridge to safety. But when I put some muscle into it, the table shifted instead. Lienna jolted, arms waving for balance.

"Damn it," I snarled. "What—"

"Kit!" She pointed. The corrosive potion was lapping at the bottom edge of the tabletop we stood on. How was it filling the room so fast? It should've been impossible without a fire-hydrant-quality pump!

She grabbed my jacket sleeve. "Onto the desk! Quickly!"

The desk. We could reach it if we jumped from the sofa's arm. This had somehow turned into the most terrifyingly real version of The Floor Is Lava ever.

"You first," I told her, kicking the magazines off the table. They sank with a faint splash, as though the yellow liquid was as harmless as water.

With a swift nod, she stepped onto the sofa. The potion was only halfway up the cushion, but when she dropped down on it, the plush foam dipped and yellow fluid flooded in. Black steam burst from her shoe.

Her shriek rang out as I wrenched her back off the sofa—and the potion breached the tabletop. Scooping her up in a bridal carry, I jumped onto the sofa arm. The padding shifted under my feet and I wobbled precariously. Lienna clutched my shoulders.

Bending forward, I coiled my legs and sprang again. I landed on the desktop in a skid, sending papers cascading over the edge. The crystal decanter with its ugly sunflower top fell off and landed with a splash.

"Are you okay?" I asked sharply.

Gulping, she nodded. "It didn't burn through my shoe. Just a little splashed my ankle."

I tipped her onto her feet but didn't let go of her waist as I skimmed the room with growing dread. The potion was two feet deep and rising—and we were even farther from the door. Would the potion keep flooding the room until it was completely filled? There were no vents in the ceiling. No gaps or escape routes. The only way out was through the door and we couldn't reach it.

Lienna's thoughts must've been racing in the same direction as mine, because her hands tightened into fists around the front of my shirt. I pulled her closer without thinking.

We clung to each other as liquid death crept toward our small island of safety.

"There must be a way to stop it," she whispered, a tremor in her voice. "What if it got triggered accidentally? Rigel would—"

"He'd need to disable it," I agreed urgently. "But how? An incantation? An emergency stop button? *What?*"

"I don't know!"

In almost perfect unison, we released each other, dropped into crouches, and scrabbled across the desk. I yanked open the one drawer that wasn't submerged while she felt underneath the desktop where Rigel had sat, searching for a button or switch.

The liquid continued to rise. Was it my imagination or was it gaining speed?

I shoved aside pens and staplers and whiteout bottles. Mundane office supplies filled the drawer. Nothing resembled a "stop the inevitable flood of agonizing death" trigger. I pulled out a black address book with a leather cover and tossed it on the desktop, then reached into the drawer again.

The potion rippled at the drawer's edge, then spilled over, filling the bottom. I yanked my hand away as droplets splashed my fingers. Spots of burning pain erupted on my skin and I shoved back to my feet.

Lienna jumped up too, and I didn't really think about it. I just reached for her hand. She grabbed it, fingers squeezing hard. The potion lapped at the desktop. Too soon. We needed to figure this out. We needed more time. We needed *something*.

A trembling inhalation rushed through her lungs. Were we going to die here? What a freakin' awful way to go. Dissolved in acid from the feet up. Goddamn Rigel and his sick mind.

Jaw clenching, I grabbed Lienna by the waist. She yipped in surprise as I lifted her off the desk and up to the cabinets. Scrambling on top of them, she crawled into the low gap under the ceiling.

I stood on the desk, chest tight, lungs straining to get enough air to my panicked brain. The potion curled over the desktop's edge.

Lienna's pale face angled toward me. "Get up here, Kit!"

"I won't fit." The gap was too small. She barely fit on her own.

"Do it!" she yelled.

Potion rushed across the desktop, and I jumped for the cabinet. I hauled myself up and into the cramped space. She flattened herself down as I slid on top of her, my back against the ceiling.

Breathing hard, I peered down at her. "Why did you roll over?"

Fear hazed her brown eyes. "Huh?"

"You were lying on your stomach a second ago."

And now she was on her back, so we were pressed front to front. Her soft chest pushed against mine with each frantic breath she took, my knees on either side of hers, my elbows braced beside her shoulders.

She blinked, then scowled. "I didn't—it just happened."

"Yeah, okay."

We stared at each other, our noses inches apart, as the lethal potion climbed the cabinet.

"I'm sorry," I whispered. "I shouldn't have brought us down here."

"I'm sorry too. I shouldn't have touched anything." She swallowed. "Kit, I'm also sorry for—"

She broke off with an airless *pffff* as my weight came down on her. I barely noticed as I leaned sideways, my stare locked on an object bobbing in the rising potion.

The crystal decanter, filled with what I had assumed was red wine.

Nothing else in the room was floating—everything else had sunk or dissolved immediately. But even more suspect was that gaudy sunflower stopper, which was the same shade of yellow as the potion.

"That's it!" I gasped. "The decanter is full of a potion that will save us!"

"What?" she yelped. "How do you know it'll—"

"I don't know, but we need to try!" I pushed up on one elbow, straining for a better look. The decanter was bobbing in the vicinity of the submerged desk, too far for me to grab. "Shit, how will we get it?"

"Can you support me?"

It took us a minute too long to rearrange our bodies in the cramped space. The rippling potion was barely six inches below the cabinet top as she stretched out across the deadly fluid. I braced as best I could against the cabinet, her legs pinned under my stomach and my hands gripping her waist as I supported her lower body.

The only thing keeping her head and shoulders out of the potion was her own upper body strength. She stretched her arm out, the decanter floating just out of reach.

"Almost," she gasped. "A little more …"

Muscles burned in my arms, and my back was cramping from the awkward pose. She stretched farther, pushing with her legs. My hands slid from her waist to her hips.

"Lienna," I gasped.

Her fingers brushed the sunflower top. "Almost—"

"I can't hold you."

"Almost," she breathed.

She pushed farther from the cabinet and I locked every muscle in my body as her center of gravity changed. My fingers bit into her hips.

"*Lienna!*"

She lunged to grab the decanter and I hauled her backward—but it wasn't enough. We were pitching off the edge and I couldn't stop it. As I fell, I shoved her toward the cabinet, red liquid spilling from the decanter in her hand.

I hit the pool of yellow potion with a splash and plunged under.

Cool fluid surrounded me. No pain. No burning. No flesh melting. I flailed my limbs, found the submerged desk, and got my feet on it. I stood, my torso bursting from the potion.

My ears filled with a horrified scream.

Lienna's cry cut off a second after I reappeared from the pool. I blinked up at her, sprawled on top of the cabinet with one hand stretched out as though she'd tried to catch me. The empty decanter floated on its side a few feet away, jostled by the waves from my fall and reappearance.

"Kit?" she whispered.

I blinked again, wondering if I was imagining the tears in her eyes. "I'm okay. You dumped the antidote in here in the nick of time."

Lifting my arm out of the now harmless potion lapping at my waist, I gave a third blink. The moment my skin parted ways with the liquid, it was dry. Not a speck of lemony potion clung to my hand. My unsubmerged clothes were dry too.

Now that the potion wasn't trying to murder us, it was actually pretty nifty.

"Oh." Lienna retracted her arm in a sheepish way. "That's g-good."

It *was* good. In fact, it was freaking amazing—and a relief-fueled grin stretched my lips. A semi-giddy laugh escaped me.

"We did it! Take that, Rigel, you cowardly son of a bitch!" Grin widening, I raised my arms toward Lienna in offer. "Shall we?"

She hesitated, then reached out. Her hands gripped my shoulders as I pulled her off the cabinet. Her legs splashed into the liquid—and she sank like a stone because there was no desk under her.

I heaved her up and onto the desktop, and she thumped against my chest. Her wide eyes stared up at me.

When had I wrapped my arms around her? Because that's where they were now. I had no explanation.

"You saved my life," she mumbled.

"Technically not. You'd already de-acidified the potion."

"But you didn't know that."

I twitched my shoulders in a shrug. "I wasn't going to let you die if I could help it."

"But you could've escaped custody."

My eyebrows scrunched. "Seriously? I know you don't like me, but do you really think I'm that much of a heartless scumbag?"

She muttered something. All I caught was "like you."

I let my arms fall from around her. For a second, she didn't move—leaning against me, her hands resting on my chest—then jerked away from me as though only just realizing how close we were. I shifted backward and the heel of my shoe landed on something.

With a considering look at the potion's rippling surface, I ducked under. Eyes squeezed shut as the cool liquid engulfed my head, I felt blindly around my feet. My hands found a leather book, and I shot back up with a splash.

"What did you do that for?" Lienna demanded.

Smirking, I held up the small black address book I'd found in the desk drawer while searching for a way not to die. Like all of Rigel's belongings, it'd escaped its potion-dunking without damage. The booby trap had been for the sole purpose of melting trespassers and all evidence of their intrusion.

I tossed the book to her. "After all that, we shouldn't leave empty-handed."

She caught it, surprise flickering over her features, before sliding the book into her satchel. "Should we get out of here?"

"You got it," I replied—and swept her off her feet again.

"Kit!"

I stepped off the desk. We plunged down, the liquid rising to my chin. I boosted her up so her head was above mine, my arms folded under her ass and her legs around my waist.

She gripped my shoulders, her satchel bouncing against her arm. "What are you doing?"

"Did you want to swim?" I started across the room in an awkward underwater gait. "Maybe you do. This is a once in a lifetime opportunity to go diving in melted lemon gelato."

I started to loosen my hold on her—and she clamped her arms around my neck in a death grip.

Squashing a smile, I carried her across the room, through the door, and into the flooded stairwell. After stubbing my toe on the first step, I carried her up to the ground level and out into the burnt remains of the office. We emerged dry without a speck of potion on us. Crazy.

I let her slide down my front until her feet landed gently on the floor. Her hands were still on my shoulders, and as she peeked up at me through dark locks of hair tangled across her face, a pink flush tinged her cheeks, scarcely discernible in the dim light.

That faint glow transformed to a bright beam that hit our faces, and a voice called loudly, "You're back!"

Lienna sprang away from me.

Security guard Trevor Eggert and his disgruntled upper lipholstry were making a beeline for us across the rubble-strewn floor, a flashlight in one hand and his cell in the other.

He waved his phone. "I've been doing some reading here, and I can't find anything about any MPD agency."

I was honestly impressed that old man Eggert knew how to use the internet. "Did you ask Siri or Alexa?"

His brow furrowed and his mustache twitched. "I Googled it. And all I can find here are conspiracies about magic."

Tugging her jacket straight, Lienna strode toward the door, radiating her usual amount of commanding agent confidence now that we were away from the secret death room. I followed on her heels, Eggert trotting after us.

"Magic, that's what this says," he reiterated, waving his phone again. "Apparently, there are real magic people here among us. And apparently, there are magic police who keep the whole thing quiet. And that got me thinking here, you see, MPD. Magic Police Department. That makes sense, doesn't it?"

I glanced over my shoulder at him. "Nothing about what you're saying makes sense, Eggsy."

"But—"

"Listen to yourself. Magic police?" We exited the building and stopped at the locked gate. "Next you're going to tell me that the Earth is flat, Kanye West is a lizard person, and Kentucky Fried Chicken's secret blend of herbs and spices is a nefarious recipe used to control the minds of the grease-eating public."

Half turning toward me, Lienna rolled her eyes. Yep, she was back to her usual self again.

"Go home, man," I told the security guard in a soothing voice. "Put on your comfy slippers, turn on the weather channel, and try not to stress about it."

"Let's go, Kit," Lienna said.

Obediently, I vaulted over the fence. She jumped over it and fell into step beside me as we walked away all casual like Riggs and Murtaugh. Eggert, standing on the other side of the fence, squinted after us.

Lienna and I crossed the rain-slicked street and got back into our trusty pocket-sized steed.

"Where to next?" I asked brightly. "Want to grab a burger to celebrate not dying? There's an awesome place down on Hastings."

She raised an eyebrow. "I'm taking you back to jail."

Damn. I'd been hoping she'd forget about that.

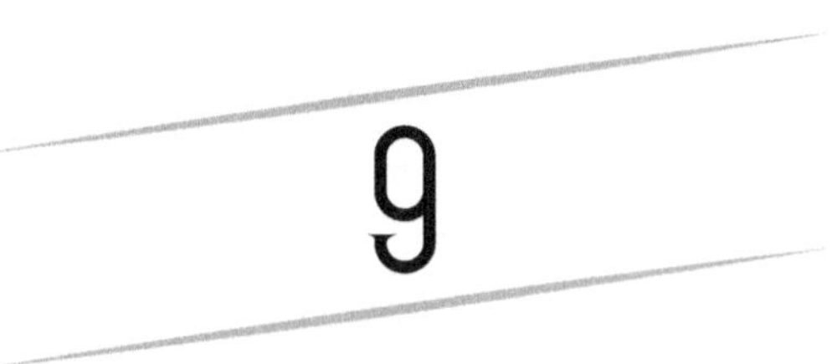

9

SPITTING RAIN pattered the windshield. I watched the wipers slash across the glass as my mind drifted through the back-to-back near-death experiences I'd scarcely survived.

Was being an MPD agent always this hazardous? If it was, Lienna had more guts than I'd thought. My KCQ employment had nothing on today. The last time I'd felt remotely safe was in Jenkins's study, picking books off his shelves and giggling over the *Kama Sutra*.

My thoughts lingered on the books, and a long breath slid from my lungs.

"You okay?"

I lifted my head, my gaze shifting to Lienna in the driver's seat. "Huh?"

"You're quiet."

"Just contemplating the timeline in *Primer*."

At my flippant tone, she returned her attention to the road. I remembered the way she'd held me as that deadly potion flooded the room. The tears in her eyes when she thought I'd died. The way she'd blushed as she stared up at me once we were safe.

Maybe she didn't hate me for being an anarchical mythic criminal flouting the MPD's benevolent rule. At least, she didn't hate me *as much*.

"Lienna …" Actually, nope. Never mind.

"What?"

"Nothing."

"What were you going to say?" she persisted.

"Forget it." It'd been a dumb idea anyway. No way she'd agree.

Taking a hand off the wheel, she lightly smacked my shoulder. "Just tell me, would you? I don't have the nerves for any more suspense."

Did she want to know that badly? I slumped in my seat. "I was going to ask if we could make one stop before you throw me back in jail."

"For burgers?" she quipped, annoyance creeping into her tone.

"No." Not that I'd ever say no to burgers. "To … my apartment."

Her brown eyes shot toward me.

"You see, rent is due in a couple of days. When I don't pay, my landlord will pitch out all my stuff. There are a few things …" I let out another heavy breath. "A few things I really don't want to lose. For, you know, the day in seventy or eighty years when MagiPol finally lets me out of prison."

Ideally, I could recover my items once I escaped custody, but I was down three for three opportunities and I wasn't sure if I'd get another one.

She eyed me suspiciously. "Where's your apartment?"

I arched an eyebrow. "Nuh-uh. Not gonna tell you that unless you agree to take me there. Otherwise, you'll just raid my shit after I'm locked up again."

"Why didn't you take this stuff with you when you fled the country?"

"Didn't have time, and also didn't know if I already had bounty hunters on my tail. I didn't want to lead them home. I was going to have my landlord mail my stuff to me."

For a price. A hefty one, knowing that greedy asshole, but I could've afforded it—before MagiPol confiscated the contents of my bank account.

She nervously ran her hands up and down the steering wheel, then blew out a breath, her hair fluttering away from her face. "Which way?"

I straightened, staring at her. "Seriously? You'll do it?"

She glared at me. "If you try *anything*, I'll teleport your limbs to the bottom of the ocean."

"Which limbs?"

"All of them."

"Oh, well, in that case … take a left here."

I directed her across downtown and into Coal Harbour, a ritzy neighborhood with towering condo buildings that overlooked long beaches and the ocean-gray inlet. We pulled into the circular drive of a particularly tall and glass-walled structure, and she parked in a visitor stall.

"You live *here?*" she asked. "No way. You're leading me into an ambush."

I pushed the door open. "Nope. This is where I live—or lived. Scout's honor."

She shut off the car, pocketed the keys, and followed me to the door with one hand in her satchel. How much did I want to bet she was holding a stun-marble, ready to fling it into my back and send me crashing into unconsciousness for a second time today?

Just inside, the doorman sat behind his desk. He glanced up at our appearance and offered a professional smile. "Welcome home, Mr. Morris."

"Thanks, Hardy. I lost my keys. Can you let me into my apartment?"

"Sure thing." Jumping up, he went ahead of us and hit the elevator call button. The doors chimed and opened. Lienna was stepping on my heels as I walked in alongside Hardy. He pressed his key fob to the panel inside, then selected the eleventh floor. The door closed, and the elevator rushed upward.

Lienna's glower singed holes in the back of my head the whole way up.

With another chime, the doors opened, and Hardy led the way down a carpeted hall with numbered doors. At 1106, he unlocked the bolt.

"Have a nice evening, Mr. Morris. And let me know if you need a new key."

"You bet," I said as he retreated toward the elevator, then pushed the door open.

The familiar scent of home, underlaid with the mustiness of a room that'd been closed up for too long, hit me hard. I walked in, sighing as my gaze traveled across the open floor plan with its spacious kitchen, large living room with a wide electric fireplace, and floor-to-ceiling windows with a view of the harbor.

"Fancy," Lienna observed acidly. "Crime pays well, doesn't it?"

I shrugged, too tired to come up with a good retort.

"Go get your things, then," she snapped. "We aren't staying."

Not bothering to remove my shoes—it wasn't like I'd ever return here to be annoyed about grit on the glossy hardwood—I headed for the short hall. Three doors waited, and I opened the center one to enter my bedroom. It was large and airy, with a king-sized bed that faced more tall windows.

I crossed to the nightstand beside the bed, but when I squatted down to reach for the low shelf at its base, Lienna appeared at my shoulder.

"Hold it!" She crouched, elbowing me aside, and peered at the contents of the shelf. Her wary squint faltered. "Those are—"

I reached past her and pulled the handful of books out. As I straightened, she shot up too, her glare undiminished.

"Books?" she said accusingly. "That's what you came for?"

"Yep."

"What's special about them? Are they valuable?"

To me, yeah. To anyone else, not one bit. "If you're worried, see for yourself."

I dumped them into her arms, taking her by surprise, then strode into the walk-in closet. Most of it was empty. My clothes were lined up along the nearest wall, neatly arranged on hangers.

As I flipped through the garments, she opened a tattered copy of *The Adventures of Huckleberry Finn*, frowning at the expected and mundane story inside. When she looked up again, I was halfway out of my shirt.

"What are you doing?" she asked shrilly.

"Changing. Clean clothes. It's nice, you know?" I pulled the shirt over my head, dropped it on the floor, and shook out a dark blue tee. "I can enjoy it for a few minutes before I'm back in a jumpsuit."

Her mouth opened and closed as I slid on the clean shirt, tugged the hem down, then toed off my shoes. When I unbuckled my belt, her stare jumped back to the books she held. She raised the Mark Twain paperback and frowned at the leather-bound Bible beneath it.

"I thought you weren't religious," she began, lifting her gaze—right as I pushed the MPD-issued torture-boxers down my hips.

Her eyes bulged, and I almost snorted. I was pretty sure she looked away before spotting the goods, but she still wobbled with bashful shock as though I'd started pole dancing. The stack of books she held tipped dangerously.

"Don't drop those," I warned as I slid on a clean pair of boxer-briefs. Ah, so much better. "And I'm not religious."

"Then why do you have a Bible?" she asked, staring at the floor, cheeks flaming.

I stepped into a pair of worn, extra-comfy jeans. "Because it was special to someone else."

"Who?"

Instead of answering, I fed my belt through the new jeans and buckled it, then stuffed my feet back into my shoes. Brushing past her, I returned to the bedroom and paused beside the bed. The scent of laundry detergent filled my nose, making my chest ache. Clean laundry was the smell of home.

Whether I escaped MPD custody or not, it'd be a long time before I got to enjoy the scent, or the feeling, of a home again.

"What else do you want to take?" Lienna asked, following me out of the closet.

"Nothing. That's it."

Her frown returned, more doubtful than suspicious this time.

I glanced at her, then pitched forward onto the bed. My face hit the thick comforter and I groaned.

"What are you doing?"

I rolled the rest of the way onto the mattress and flopped onto my back, one arm across my eyes. "Do you know what those jail cell cots are like? This is the last bed I'll get to lie on for … years. Just give me a minute to memorize the feeling."

Silence answered me. After a moment, the mattress dipped. I peeked under my arm to find Lienna sitting on the corner of the bed, gazing around with a wrinkle between her brows.

"This just isn't the sort of place I imagined you'd live in," she muttered.

"Me neither. This is ten times fancier than anywhere else I've ever lived." I covered my eyes again. "Rigel recommended it. I think his buddy owns the place. I got a good deal, and KCQ paid well."

"Ah, yes. The spoils of fraud and theft."

"'Suppose so."

Her voice went even icier. "Do you even care that you were cheating people?"

I thought of the books in her arms, then nestled back into the comforter and breathed in the scent of home. "Being a mythic crook is better than being a human freak."

"You aren't a human."

"Didn't know I was a mythic, remember? KCQ found me. They taught me about magic."

The mattress creaked as she shifted. "I understand that, but once you realized they were criminals, you … you should've left the guild."

I cracked my eyes open, but all I could see was my arm, resting on my forehead. This weird sharing mood of mine was waning, but I'd blabbed enough mush that I might as well finish with the truth.

"I've never fit in anywhere. People don't want me around. I make them uncomfortable … scare them. Everywhere I ever went, everyone wanted to get rid of me—until Rigel invited me to his guild. There, I wasn't just welcome … I was useful. I was part of the team." I let out a short, harsh breath. "So to answer your question, no, I didn't care what the guild was really doing. Not enough to leave."

The bed bounced again. A soft footstep, then a warm hand tugged on my wrist, lifting my arm. Lienna leaned over me, peering into my eyes.

"Kit … you …" She struggled for words, lips pursing with thought.

I watched her soft lips, surprised by how entrancing they were.

Her gaze searched my face, and that faint blush reappeared. She abruptly straightened. "You broke the law. But … but if you help catch Quentin, I'll do whatever I can to minimize the charges against you."

"What can you do?"

"I'm not sure." Her eyes blazed. "But I'll figure it out."

An odd tightness constricted my throat—and I realized I believed her. I believed she would help me.

Wow, I was *really* going mushy. It had to be the bed. It was hard to be jaded while lying on a slice of cumulus heaven. Before I lost my grip on reality, I sat up. Lienna moved aside as I slid off the mattress.

"I guess we can go now." My focus settled on the books tucked under her arm. "But those … I need to stash them somewhere safe."

If they went back to the precinct with me, I'd never see them again. Damn it. Why hadn't I thought of that earlier?

Lienna hefted the small pile. "I … I can hold on to them for you. For the time being."

My eyes narrowed. "You're taking my belongings hostage?"

"No, I'm offering to care for them until you—until you're ready to take them back."

"They're mementos, not grimoires. You won't find anything in them that you can use to—"

"I'm trying to be nice!" she cut in. "You saved my life and I want to do something nice for you!"

Doubt flitted through me, but she was giving me that fierce stare, and instead of accusatory and condemning—like most of her glares—it was … I didn't know, but it poked at the part of me that wanted to believe her.

"Okay," I conceded. Not like I had any better options anyway. "Thank you."

The stern downward tilt to her mouth softened into a smile. A real one. An actual nice smile.

Musing over her offer to care for my books, I scooped them out of her arms and left the bedroom. With a longing glance across the living room, I headed for the door.

"Kit." She lingered beside my seventy-inch flat-screen television—one of the few items I'd purchased for the apartment. "Are you sure there isn't anything else you want to save?"

I shook my head. "None of this is mine. The apartment came furnished."

Frowning, she crouched beside the TV stand. "What about these?"

I drifted back to her side and peered at the shelves—lined with the spines of DVD and Blu-ray cases. I sank down, sitting on my heels.

"I collected them after starting with KCQ. I always wanted a movie collection, but I could never afford …" I coughed. "But yeah, none of those are rare or anything. I can find them all again if—if I get the chance," I finished lamely.

Not likely, considering I was doomed to either a life on the run or a life behind bars.

Lienna ran her finger across a large assortment of goofy comedies, including the entire *Monty Python* collection, before landing on my copy of *Casablanca*.

"Ooh," I murmured. "Classic."

She pulled it off the shelf. "I've never seen it."

"Seriously? Everyone should see *Casablanca*."

"Hmm." She examined the illustration of Ingrid Bergman and Humphrey Bogart dramatically pressed together on the cover. "It looks kind of …"

"Don't you dare say boring. This is the most beautiful movie ever made."

She raised a skeptical eyebrow.

"It is!" As her eyebrow rose higher, I stepped back my enthusiasm, oddly embarrassed. "It's about being part of something bigger than yourself. I think there's beauty in that."

Her lower lip caught between her teeth. "Maybe …" She seemed to hang on the word. "Maybe we should watch it."

Snorting, I pushed back to my feet. "Sure. You can download it on your phone, then stand outside my cell and I'll watch it over your shoulder."

She stayed crouched, still holding the movie. "I mean right now."

I froze halfway through a step toward the door and peered down at the top of her head. "Why? You want to make sure it's actually a movie and not a disc storing all my criminal secrets?"

"No, I just—" She abruptly stood, avoiding my eyes. "Never mind."

She started to set the DVD case on the TV stand, but I caught her wrist. "Are you serious? You want to watch *Casablanca* right now? Here in my apartment?"

She muttered something, her cheeks tinged with pink.

"Sorry?"

"I said we don't need to rush back to the precinct." She half-heartedly tugged her wrist away, but I didn't let go. "It's already late, and the investigation won't resume until morning. It might be a while before you can rebuild your collection, so … so why not enjoy it one more time?"

I let her withdraw her arm from beneath my hand. She glanced up warily and seemed surprised to find me staring back with equal wariness.

"What?" she huffed defensively. "It was just an idea."

"I …" Shaking my head, I admitted the truth. "I can't tell if you're tricking me."

"Tricking you?"

"Yeah. You know, getting me all excited about an illegal movie night, waiting for the opening credits, then slapping on the cuffs and dragging me out amidst your nefarious laughter."

She blinked twice—then rolled those big brown eyes so forcefully her head tipped back. She slapped the DVD case against my chest.

"Put the movie on, Kit."

With that, she swept over to the sofa, dropped onto the cushions, and folded her arms expectantly.

Holy shit. She was serious.

A hesitant smile pulled at my lips. "Should I make some popcorn?"

Two and a half minutes later, I sat beside her with a big bowl of popcorn balanced on one hand and the remote in my other hand. She plucked a fluffy, buttery bit of popcorn out and tossed it in her mouth.

I tried not to stare.

The opening narration played, and my unease slid away as the screen filled with a slowly spinning black-and-white globe, the camera focusing on North Africa.

"When was this made?" she asked, scooping more popcorn from the bowl.

"1942. It's a movie set in the middle of World War II, filmed and released in the middle of World War II. They shot it five months after Pearl Harbor."

She made a quiet noise of interest and settled back to watch. We finished the popcorn and I slid the bowl onto the end table. As I shifted back to my spot, the cushions dipped. My arm brushed hers, but she didn't look away from the television.

I resisted the urge to provide commentary, letting the movie pull her in, but when the crowd in Rick's bar began to sing "La Marseillaise" to drown out a group of Nazi soldiers performing a German anthem, I couldn't help myself.

Leaning toward her, our arms pressed together, I whispered, "Watch the extras who are singing."

She squinted at the screen. "Is that woman crying?"

"A bunch of the extras were war refugees. They escaped Nazi persecution in Europe, ran away to America, and ended up singing about it in *Casablanca*. This was real for them."

"Wow," she said softly.

By the time we got to the climactic scene between Rick and Ilsa in the rain at the airport, I was in full Bogart mode, quoting his best lines alongside him. Lienna's gaze flicked between me and the TV, the corners of her mouth twitching with each line I delivered.

At just the right moment, following Bogart's cue, I touched my fingers to her chin and in my best melodramatic baritone murmured, "Here's lookin' at you, kid."

For a single heartbeat, she stared at me with wide eyes—then burst into laughter and swatted my hand away. "You made me miss it!"

"Whoops." Grinning, I grabbed the remote to back the movie up. "I promise not to distract you—for the next thirty seconds."

She laughed again, adding one of her patented eye rolls. Her amusement cracked her defensive agent mask, giving me a better look at the woman hidden beneath it—and gotta be honest here, I kind of thought I might like the person I saw.

That unfortunate feeling would probably bite me in the ass sooner or later.

IO

I climbed onto the top bunk and collapsed. Rolling onto my back, I adjusted my gray jumpsuit until it was moderately close to comfortable, missing my t-shirt and jeans like crazy. And my king-sized bed. They didn't design either these jumpsuits or jail cells with coziness in mind.

Duncan was leaning against the wall across from the bunk bed, staring at me. My hair was slick from the rain, which had caught his attention.

"A little bit," I answered, trying to sound like this was a totally normal conversation to have in a jail cell.

"Yeah?" Eyes bright, he stepped away from the wall—and closer to the bunk.

Please don't touch me, please don't touch me, please don't touch me. "Yup."

"What was it like?"

What was he looking for here? Some adjective-laden description of the water cascading from the heavens? Should I write a haiku?

I sighed. "I don't know, Duncan. It was raining from the sky. It was kind of wet."

His expression flattened at my dry response, and he leaned against the wall again. "Did you have fun on your field trip? I heard they have you out there hunting your best friend."

Word got around the MagiPol holding cells.

"Quentin's not my best friend," I replied. "Don't tell me you wouldn't jump at the chance to get out of here if they offered it to you."

The hydromage shrugged. "Maybe, maybe not. I know I wouldn't find it so easy to cooperate with the MPD. That's for sure."

"You might," I said, "if it gave you the opportunity to escape."

He shook his head skeptically and disappeared onto the lower bunk, the metal frame shuddering. "And look how well that worked out for you."

I inhaled slowly. He had a point. It wasn't as though Lienna had strapped me to a prison gurney like Hannibal Lecter.

Still, my chances for escape hadn't been top-notch. That had never stopped me before—when I was nine years old, I jumped out of a fifth-story window and into a snowbank to avoid getting the belt from my douchebag of a foster father—but though I'd been watching for my chance with Lienna, it hadn't happened.

Part of that was an unwillingness to risk my entire future on anything less than a sure-fire opportunity, which Lienna wasn't likely to give me—not unless I was willing to seriously hurt her. For example, shoving her into a vat of flesh-eating potion.

But a guy had to draw the line somewhere. Besides, if I betrayed her like that, she'd probably return from the dead to smite me with her abjuration voodoo.

We were nowhere near catching Quentin yet. I'd have more opportunities before the looming date of my sentencing—or maybe I wouldn't need to book it. If I earned enough brownie points with Blythe, and if Lienna came through on her promise to help me …

I rubbed a hand over my face. Was I seriously considering putting my future in Lienna's and Blythe's law-abiding and judgmental hands? Was I actually thinking that facing my sentencing might be the better option?

What had gotten into me?

Rolling onto my stomach, I stuck my head over the edge of the bunk to peer at Duncan, who seemed to be swishing saliva around in his mouth.

"Did you get one of those sentencing summons?" I asked him.

"Yeah. June fourteenth."

"Same date as mine."

He gargled his spit, then swallowed it. "They're probably scheduling all the serious stuff on the same day, so the Judiciary Council can get through it all in one go."

All the serious stuff? They were lumping me in with this lunatic? Since when was interning at an unscrupulous law firm equivalent to *killing seventeen human beings*?

"How many charges do you have?" I asked.

"Seventeen. Obviously. You?"

"Sixty-one."

"That's a lot."

No. Shit. Sherlock.

"Do you have any idea how many years I'm looking at?" Not that I expected a real answer from a guy on the Ed Gein end of the sanity spectrum.

"Hard to say with these people."

"Well, how many do you think you'll get?" There's no way my total sentence would be greater than this water-working psychopath's.

"Oh, I won't be serving any time."

"Bullshit," I snapped, wondering how he could be that delusional. "You're getting life, man. No way you aren't."

"Are you that thick, kid?" he snorted. "I'm getting the death sentence."

His matter-of-fact tone dumbfounded me. "What? Are you sure?"

"Well, you can never be sure when it comes to the MPD, but yeah, I'm pretty sure. And they don't wait around, you know. When you get the death sentence, I think they give you, I dunno … two weeks? Then …" He drew a finger across his neck, adding a lovely sound effect with the gesture.

"Oh … I see."

I rolled back onto my mattress and stared unblinkingly at the ceiling. Sixty-one charges. Was that enough to earn me a death sentence? It seemed unlikely, especially with Lienna's tip about an unknown number of those charges being flimsier than cardboard in the rain.

But like Duncan had said, you could never be sure with the MPD.

All things considered, proceeding with my hearing and getting a short sentence was better than a fugitive's life—as much as a Harrison Ford/Tommy Lee Jones style game of cat and mouse sounded awesome—but if the worst-case scenario was *execution*, then no thanks. Option B was officially off the table.

Lienna's quietly pleased smile appeared in my mind's eye, but I shoved it away and tried to calculate how many hours I had until my sentencing. I gave up when I realized I didn't know what time it was. The number was less than three hundred, though. Less than three hundred hours to escape.

And if I failed to make a proper getaway, I might find myself following Duncan the Douser into the field out back, where the MPD would put us down like Old Yeller.

CONTROLLING MY BREATHING, I tightened my core. Forearms braced on the floor, my cot's thin blanket acting as a yoga mat, I held my body nearly vertical, legs in the air and knees bent, my feet curling down toward my head. Sweat ran down my spine to the nape of my neck as I drew in a slow breath, muscles burning.

"What's this one called?" Duncan asked in a bored tone, reclining on the bunk with his ankles crossed.

"Scorpion pose," I puffed as I let my spine bend more, coiling my torso in a tight backward arch. All sorts of muscles and joints pulled taut.

"Doesn't look that hard."

Yeah, sure. Duncan wouldn't even be able to hold himself up.

Despite my existential anxiety, I'd slept most of the night—battling telekinetics and escaping alchemical booby traps was exhausting. But I'd woken stiff and achy, and a long, boring morning spent lounging on my hard cot hadn't helped. My solution? A limb-stretching, muscle-busting yoga routine.

By the way, if anyone ever tells you yoga is just a bunch of sissy stretches for girls, go ahead and call them an idiot.

With a final breath, I uncurled my body back to vertical, then lowered my feet to the floor. Sitting back on my heels, I wiped my hand across my forehead. A trickle of sweat ran down to my jaw.

Duncan's beady little eyes tracked its journey and I shuddered.

Turning so he wasn't in my direct line of sight, I adjusted the knot of my jumpsuit's sleeves, ensuring it wouldn't impede my next pose. Since the MPD couldn't be bothered to supply either workout clothes or a spare jumpsuit, I'd pulled the top half down and tied it around my waist so it wouldn't soak up too much sweat, leaving my torso naked.

As I prepared to assume the eight-angle pose, someone rapped on our cell door. Well, if it wasn't Superbeard the Woodchopping Agent with the greatest name on the planet.

He jangled a pair of those goddamn magic handcuffs. "The captain wants to see you."

"Now?"

"Obviously now."

Torn between annoyance and the near-frantic hope that I was about to experience my next—and if all went well, my last—out-of-prison excursion, I got to my feet.

Duncan tossed a smirk my way. "Gonna go play with the pretty rookie again?"

"Or maybe Blythe has decided to chop me up into tiny pieces to use as vampire bait."

"I guess you'll find out."

Cool. Thanks.

Superbeard unlocked the cell and gestured me out into the hallway. I reached for the knot of fabric around my waist—but my skin was slick with perspiration and I didn't want to gross up my only garment. With no better option, I walked out as I was.

The agent glowered. "Dress properly."

"Dude, I was mid-workout. Give me a minute to cool off."

"Once I cuff you, you won't be able to put it on."

I shrugged.

Losing patience, he snapped the cuffs on and led me to the same old interrogation room. A moment later, I was uncomfortably seated on the same old chair, with the same old cuffs chained to the same old table. The door slammed behind my escort.

I leaned against the chair, the metal pressing against my bare back. Yikes, cold.

The door flew open again almost immediately. Lienna breezed in with purpose, spotted me, and lurched to a halt with her jaw hanging open. Marching in the rookie's wake, Blythe bumped into her back.

"Agent Shen! Would you—" Blythe spotted me. "Morris!"

"Yes?" I inquired innocently.

"Why aren't you dressed?"

"I was busy when Agent Wood Chipper came calling."

Lienna's cheeks flushed. Catching her eye, I arched my eyebrows—and her blush deepened.

"Exercising," I added as I pulled my hands up, chains clanking, and awkwardly pushed a few strands of damp hair off my forehead. "But if I had any clue when to expect our special dates, I could primp up nice and proper for you ladies."

Blythe stomped to the table, carrying an armload of files with a side of extra-spicy mean sauce. She dropped the stack on the table with a loud thump, and several folders slid off the pile and onto the floor.

"You dropped a couple of the—" I began helpfully.

"Put your shirt on."

"It's not a shirt. It's a jumpsuit. And sure." I jangled my cuffs pointedly.

She glanced from my wrists to my torso, then sank into the seat across from me, kicking a folder in the process.

I tried again. "You dropped—"

"I don't want to be here," she snapped. "I want you to be very aware of that. Do you understand me, Mr. Morris?"

"I think so," I replied, even though I didn't. I mean, I know I'm not The Rock, but my pecs couldn't be *that* offensive. "Where would you rather be?"

"Interviewing your cohorts has proven exceedingly frustrating. So, despite wanting to be anywhere else, I am here so you can answer my questions."

"Ah. You went through Rigel's address book."

She shoved her hand into the stack of files on the table, pulled out the book, and tossed it at me. Thanks to my cuffed wrists, I missed the catch and it smacked against my bare chest.

Lienna made a muffled, rather strange sound in the back of her throat. I glanced at her—standing beside the closed door with her mouth pressed into an intense scowl, as though scowling would cancel out her blush—then fished the book off my lap.

"Look at the entry for Hilda Mills," Blythe ordered.

I flipped through the alphabetically organized names until I got to the 'M' section: Hilda Mills, mentalist. There was a phone number and email address, and in the margin beside her name, Rigel had scrawled the letters "BS."

I smirked. Mills was a new, freshly minted lawyer known for her skillful bullshitting.

"BS," Blythe said. "Blue Smoke."

Oh. Right. I nodded as though that was absolutely what I'd been thinking. "I see that."

"We found nine names with the same annotation. One is Quentin, and we have five others in custody—the two telekinetics who attacked you and Agent Shen yesterday, and three who were arrested with the fall of the guild."

"Which three?" I asked. Who had Rigel brought into his top-secret clubhouse meetings? Geoff and Jeff didn't set the bar high for inclusion and I wanted to know who else had gotten an invitation instead of me.

"It doesn't matter. They aren't talking."

"I thought you had ways to make captives talk."

The captain's eyes flared, but before she could threaten me with a classic abuse of power, Lienna cleared her throat.

"We need to locate the remaining three." She dared to step closer to my unclothed man muscles. "If Quentin's trying to do something related to Blue Smoke, we have to assume he'll contact them."

"And you want me to give them to you."

Blythe pulled three folders out of the stack and laid them in front of me one by one. "Collin Sharpe. Nazario Valdez. Maggie Cook."

I knew all three but didn't let on. The ball was in my court and I needed to decide what shot to play.

Quentin had told me Rigel kept members of Blue Smoke in the dark about who their coconspirators were, but if my empathic friend had made it to the underground lair before us and gone through Rigel's stuff, he probably knew about Collin, Nazario, and Maggie.

So, which one would he track down first? Impossible to guess without knowing what he was trying to accomplish. He might even have doubts about his plans, based on his desire to visit the Kitsilano Klairvoyant. Or he'd *had* doubts. Jenkins had suggested Quentin's reading was a positive one.

What was the line Jenkins had revealed? Something disparaging about women and … cigar smoke, wasn't it?

I looked up at Lienna. "Do you have your phone on you?"

Her stare jerked up to my face, and my eyebrows rose by the same margin. Just where had she been looking?

"Why?" she asked with another throat clearing.

"Look up that poem from Quentin's diviner reading. It was by the guy who wrote *The Jungle Book*."

As she pulled out her cell phone, Blythe scowled. "What's the point of this? I'm not centering my investigation around a diviner's reading."

"Even if you don't believe in his reading, Quentin does."

"Listen to this," Lienna said, eyes glued to her phone. "'A million surplus Maggies are willing to bear the yoke; and a woman is only a woman, but a good cigar is a smoke.'"

Holy shit, that was even better than I'd thought. I tapped the folder with Maggie Cook's name on it. "I think we know who Quentin is looking for."

Blythe swept the other two folders back into the pile and opened the remaining one. "Maggie Cook. Arcana. Thirty-five years old. Smoke and Mirrors guild."

Lienna frowned. "She's not a KCQ member?"

"No, which is why she escaped our original roundup."

Escaped? Was she a criminal by default, just because her name was in a dead man's address book?

"She isn't a rogue," I muttered. "She's a good person."

"And you're a preeminent judge of what makes a person good?" Blythe scoffed. "The sixty-one charges against you suggest otherwise."

Lienna shifted her feet. "Captain Blythe, I told you he saved my life yesterday."

She'd actually told the steely precinct captain how her prisoner-assistant had saved her? I'd figured that'd be an embarrassing mishap she'd rather leave out of her report. And also, I hadn't saved her. She'd already nullified the potion's deadly properties by the time I made my shameful act of heroism.

Blythe's lips thinned. "I'll be reviewing that incident in further detail. And you'd do well to remember that manipulation is second nature to his kind."

Stiffening, Lienna crossed her arms. "I don't think Kit is cut from the same cloth as the other KCQ rogues. In light of their corrupting influence over his entry into the mythic community, his charges should be reviewed and—"

"Enough." Blythe slapped Maggie Cook's folder down on the table. "I'll decide if Mr. Morris earns leniency. Your job is to apprehend Quentin Bianchi."

Lienna's jaw tightened. Her shoulders shifted as she inhaled deeply, then she turned to me. "What can you tell us about Maggie? We sent agents to her home, workplace, and guild, but no one can find her."

I swallowed back a flippant retort and answered seriously— or as serious as I ever got, "She probably caught a whiff of those agents and decided to lie low."

"Clearly the behavior of an innocent woman," Blythe observed. "If she didn't do anything wrong, she has no reason to hide."

"Oh yeah, no reason at all, even though you'd arrest her based on basically nothing." I stuffed down my rising temper. "But Maggie's also on the paranoid side, so she wouldn't sit around after what happened to Rigel."

"What's her relationship with Rigel?" Blythe asked.

"Freelancer. Rigel hired a lot of freelancers."

"Can you put us in touch with her?"

"It won't be that easy."

"Why not?"

"Like I said, she's paranoid. She won't willingly talk to scary MPD agents."

"I suppose you have a better idea." Lienna hadn't rolled her eyes during this interrogation yet, but I could tell she was prepared to. The eye roll was loaded, like a bullet in the chamber of a gun, ready to be fired.

"Sure do, but it'll only work if you pocket your abjuration magic for a few minutes and let me use *my* magic."

She pulled the trigger on that eye roll. It was a doozy. Her pupils completely disappeared behind her eyelids.

I kept my expression vaguely amused, revealing none of my tension. I'd spent the night and most of my day ruminating on the revelation that execution could become an unavoidable stop on my sentencing journey. My conclusion? I could no longer wait for an opportunity to escape.

It was time to make that opportunity happen.

Blythe snorted with derision almost on par with Lienna's. "What makes you think I'd ever allow that?"

Bracing my elbows on the table, I propped my chin on my hands and grinned. Oh, she would. Once I explained my "plan," she wouldn't be able to resist giving her permission.

What I wasn't going to tell the captain, however, was that I didn't intend to allow the MPD to arrest Maggie Cook any more than I intended to ever set foot in this precinct again.

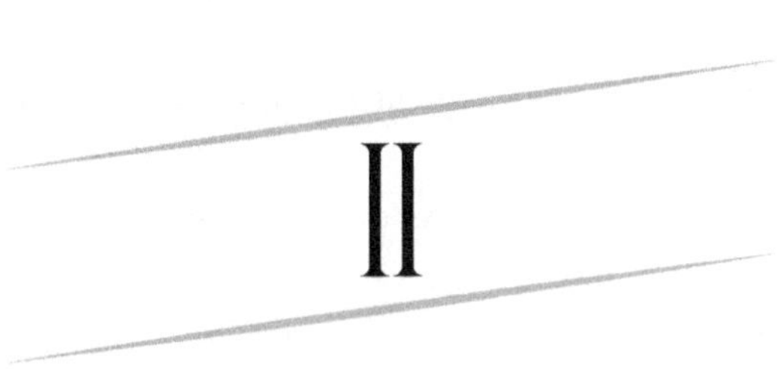

II

"**SHOW ME.**" Lienna had her arms crossed, a nervous set to her jaw.

I raised an eyebrow. "Show you what?"

"What you're going to do. I want to see it before she shows up."

Lienna, Agent Jack Cutter, and I were seated at a small table near the entrance of an independent café in Mount Pleasant. A handful of patrons loitered at small tables among stark white, minimalistic décor that Maggie would hate.

That was the problem. Maggie was one of my favorite people, but she was notoriously picky about shit like this. If she got the wrong vibes from a place, she wouldn't set foot in it. The first time we ever met for coffee—or tea, in her case—we'd tried three cafés before she approved of one.

This place's minimalist style was antithetical to Maggie's splashy, vintage aesthetic—but the location worked very well for *my* plan. So, to get Maggie in here, I would have to do some Redecorating. With a capital R.

I pointed at Lienna's anti-magic cat's eye necklace. "You'll have to take that off."

She hesitated. "If you try to pull anything …"

"You'll wreak untold horrors upon my flesh until I wish I was never born?"

"No." She flicked her hand at Agent Cutter, who shot me a menacing grin. "He will."

Agent Cutter's magic wasn't as scary as Lienna's, if I were to believe her interdimensional threats, but he was a telethesian—basically, a psychic bloodhound. The subtext was clear: escape was not an option.

"And I have a holding artifact that I've been told is extremely unpleasant," the lumberjack added.

Ah, that was the scary part. I've never experienced a holding spell firsthand, but I know they freeze the victim in place, rendering them utterly incapable of any movement aside from shallow breathing and the odd blink … if they're lucky. Unpleasant indeed.

"Don't worry," I said. "I won't do anything stupid."

Not yet, anyway.

With slow movements, as though I might lunge across the table, Lienna raised the cat's eye necklace over her head. Laying it carefully on the tabletop, she gave me the go-ahead nod.

I took off the shark-tooth necklace and dropped it beside hers, concealing my relieved sigh with a showy throat clear. As her petite nose scrunched suspiciously, I focused on the glimmer in my brain that was her mind—her essence, brainwaves, whatever. I don't have legit *terms* for this shit. I just follow my instincts.

Getting a nice, good focus on her, I changed the café's walls from clinical white to a warm muddy brown.

Lienna's eyes bulged, but no one else in the café even blinked.

Humming the *Jeopardy* tune, I morphed the linoleum floor to rustic hardwood, then changed the counters to match. How about an assortment of kitschy paintings I'd seen in a Wes Anderson movie for the walls? Sure, add those. A bobblehead of Ruth Bader Ginsburg appeared beside the espresso machine. For flavor, I added an old jukebox in the back corner, then finished it off by warming the hue of the lights and dimming them enough to make things cozy.

"What do you think?" I asked.

Lienna's wide eyes bounced around the redecorated space. "No one else can see this?"

"Just you."

Truth be told, I *could* make everyone around us see what she was seeing, but I had zero plans to share that tidbit. First, suddenly altering every customer's perception would cause a certain amount of alarm. Second, it was more difficult. And third, both Lienna and Agent Cutter were on a "need to know" basis regarding my abilities.

And they needed to know as little as possible.

She glanced at her partner, who mumbled, "I don't see anything."

"So, it isn't an illusion?" she mused, a hint of wonder leaking into her tone.

I nodded. "More like a hallucination."

"But it looks so real. Is it limited to visual alterations?"

"Not entirely," I hedged. Visual hallucinations were the easiest, and audio hallucinations weren't too bad. I could alter smell if I needed to, but taste and touch were next-level difficult.

I let the vision die, returning Lienna's perception of the room back to its former austere glory.

She shook her head. "I've never seen a mythic do that before. I don't even know what a power like that would be called."

That made two of us.

I didn't *need* to know what my ability was called—it didn't require a label to function properly—but there was something satisfying, maybe even empowering, about putting a title on it and being able to refer to part of your identity by name.

She tapped her lower lip thoughtfully, then a small smile curved her mouth. "You really are unique, Kit. Your abilities are something else. Being able to—"

Agent Cutter gave a discreet cough, and she straightened, maybe realizing her voice had gone too warm and relaxed. Much more "movie night pals" than "agent in charge of a dangerous criminal."

"Remember," she told me sternly, "if you lose control of the situation, it's our job to take Maggie Cook in. Captain's orders."

"You got it, boss." I shifted my gaze to the window. "By the way, she's coming."

A woman in her thirties was speed-walking toward the café. She wore paint-stained overalls and a bright yellow rain slicker, but its hood didn't hide the Smurf-blue hair and oversized, thick-rimmed glasses.

Agent Cutter and Lienna scrambled off their seats. As she reached for the two necklaces, my hand shot out and I swiped them off the tabletop. Grinning, I held up her necklace, the cat's eye swinging.

She plucked it out of my hand and hurried after her temporary partner. They dropped into a booth at the back where they could keep watch over me, and she looped her anti-magic necklace over her head, the cat's eye bouncing against her chest. She caught my gaze and offered a sneaky smile of encouragement that Agent Cutter didn't notice.

I curled my hand around the second necklace, the pendant clenched in my fist.

By the time Maggie reached the door, I'd locked onto her mind. To her eyes, the café was rustic and charming instead of a poorly sterilized hospital cafeteria. A gust of chilly, wet air swept inside as she opened the door.

Now the real test of my abilities began—holding the hallucination while carrying on a perfectly natural conversation that would require its fair share of lying, manipulation, and careful questioning.

Yeah, this would be fun.

Maggie's gaze darted across every patron, checking for threats, then she scurried to my window-side table, assessing the room once more as she came.

"Hey, Kit," she greeted with a smile.

Standing, I reached out for a quick hug. "Hey, Maggie."

As my arms closed around her narrow shoulders and her odd, dusty lavender perfume tickled my nose, I quashed a nervous twist in my gut. Focus, I reminded myself. Hold the projections.

And keep my guilt tamped down real tight.

As I dropped back into my seat, she sat across from me, her eyes moving in a ceaseless search for danger. "Are you sure this place is safe?"

I made a show of peering around. "Looks safe to me."

Her shoulders relaxed imperceptibly. "It does … it does. I like this place."

Mission accomplished. Well, sort of. Making her comfortable enough to talk was only part one.

Before I could launch into part two, she smiled. "I'm glad you're safe, Kit. Very glad."

"I got lucky." Sort of true. I wasn't dead, after all.

"KCQ was bad, bad news. I'm happy you're free of them."

"You heard what happened?" I asked cautiously.

"I heard most of your people got rounded up. I heard Rigel was killed." She hesitated. "One of the Smoke and Mirrors guys heard a story about you down in LA."

As far as the public was concerned, Smoke and Mirrors was a special effects company for the movie industry, but non-mythics had no clue how special those effects were.

That's what Maggie did. Aside from whipping up ultra-safe, cool-looking explosions for major film studios, she was one of the best alchemists in the city. She could transmute almost anything, if you gave her enough time, and she had a knack for spells that involved astrology.

"That wasn't me," I lied, pressing my thumb into the pendant hidden in my lap. "It was probably another KCQ intern."

"Could be." She fiddled with one of the many rings on her fingers. "You said on the phone that you were looking for information."

"Have you heard about Quentin?"

"Yes, yes. He's on the run now. Have you talked to him??"

I shook my head. "I couldn't reach him. But I talked to Jenkins—his diviner. Quentin's mentioned him to you before, right? According to Jenkins, Quentin went to him for a reading about Blue Smoke."

Maggie blinked rapidly. "Blue Smoke. Do you know …?"

"I don't know the details," I said, mixing lies with truth, "but Rigel was going to bring me in before he kicked the bucket."

Her attention skirted around the café again. "Why? What do you want with Blue Smoke?"

I honed my focus on her mind. If I let any part of the hallucination slip—if the paint on the walls faded, or the hardwood warped, or the Ruth Bader Ginsburg bobblehead twitched unnaturally—the whole facade could fail. And that would screw up my plan in a big way.

"I'm worried about Quentin. MagiPol is all over him, and Blue Smoke is … dangerous."

"Dangerous," she repeated softly.

"Quentin is my friend. I want to help him, but I don't know enough." I leaned across the table. "You're one hell of an alchemist, and if Rigel had you freelancing for him, you must know *something* about Blue Smoke."

Swallowing, she stood from the table. "I need some tea."

While she placed her order at the counter, I glanced at the ever-vigilant pair at the back of the café. Lienna, as always, had one hand on her satchel, and the other was fidgeting with the chain of her necklace, as though reassuring herself it was firmly in place and protecting her mind.

I really wished she'd stop doing that. It was making everything that much more difficult.

Returning to the table and sliding on her chair, Maggie blew gently on her steaming tea. "I always felt you were different from the rest of the KCQ members, Kit."

I smiled. "I thought the same thing when I first saw you there."

There was no lie in that. Her boldly dyed hair, disdain for anything that resembled office attire, and warm smile had caught my attention—mainly because she'd looked as out of place in the Psychica guild as I'd felt. That unexpected kinship had led to a casual conversation that had grown into a casual friendship, one with more warmth and genuine kindness than any relationship I'd formed during my tenure with KCQ.

"They were a greedy, greedy bunch," she murmured. "Desperation may make men evil, but greed makes evil men worse."

"I've never cared about money. I was just—"

"I know, I know. You were finally in a place that accepted you. I understand. I do. But you never belonged there. You aren't the greedy type. Rigel and the others, greed was in their blood. They reached beyond the world of lawyers and contracts."

I waited for her to continue.

"Do you know Cerberus, Kit?"

"The security guild?"

"Blue Smoke was a plan to break into Cerberus."

My spine went rigid. Break into *Cerberus*? That was nuts, even by KCQ standards.

Cerberus wasn't your standard locks and alarms anti-theft company. It was a guild of security experts—the best of the best, with an arsenal of damn near unbreakable spells for keeping valuable things safe, and people paid a good hunk o' cash for their services.

"There's been a rumor for years that Cerberus is holding on to a deep, dark secret," Maggie whispered. "A dangerous artifact. Very dangerous, very powerful. The whole purpose of Blue Smoke was to steal it. I don't know where he got that name from. Blue Smoke?"

"Was he a Scott Bakula fan?"

"What?"

"Never mind." Now was not the time for stupid jokes. I peeked sideways at our two-agent audience, then hardened the hallucinations I was projecting. "So, what was the point of it all? They wanted to steal this crazy powerful artifact to do what with it?"

"I don't know, but the answer is the same no matter what." She swirled her tea in her mug. "Greed, Kit. It's always about greed."

"And you were a part of Blue Smoke?"

"No. Well, yes. At first. I helped set up protections for a vault. Rigel wanted a place to store valuable items, and he likes my alchemy over sorcery. Especially using astral keys for a door that can only be opened on a specific day."

Hmm. The murder trap in Rigel's secret lair fit the bill for Maggie's alchemy, but it wasn't what I'd call a vault. "A specific day? What do you mean?"

Her eyes lit up; she loved talking about her work. "A seal that is unassailable except on one day of the month. Once Rigel locked it, he wouldn't need to guard it, even from his own cohorts, except on that one day." She smirked. "I chose the waning third crescent moon."

"The what now?"

"The moon at one-third visibility. I'd hoped its slowly dying light might remind him of the cost of his greed."

I squeezed my temples. "So his plan was to steal this valuable artifact from Cerberus and store it in the vault? Wasn't he planning to sell the artifact? That's the Rigel thing to do, and it wouldn't require an unassailable vault."

"I don't know. As soon as he told me the vault's purpose, and that he wanted my help with the theft, I walked away." She studied the contents of her mug. "Rigel had no right to such an artifact. It belongs in the hands of someone who isn't driven by greed."

I switched from temple squeezing to rubbing my hands over my face, debating what to ask next. I didn't strictly need this information, but I wanted to cover all my bases before I began Phase Two.

"Strange ..."

I jerked my hands down to find Maggie squinting at something over my shoulder. Shit, shit, shit. Had I let part of the hallucination slip? There were a lot of pieces to keep track of and my mental energy was flagging.

"What?" I asked cautiously.

"Something feels off about this place." Her eyes resumed their paranoid dance around the room. "Are you doing something?"

Maggie knew what my abilities were. If she sensed something wasn't right, I couldn't fault her for suspecting me.

Unfortunately, her inside knowledge meant I had to work even harder to fool her. When I get distracted or fatigued, my hallucinations start to go a bit wonky, uncanny-valley style. Most people don't notice anything more than an unsettling itch in their subconscious—but those who know *why* they might be feeling that way can spot the incongruities way faster.

She pierced me with a worried stare. "Kit, what's going on?"

According to the plan I'd proposed to Blythe, this was the point where I should give Lienna and Agent Cutter the signal to move in and arrest Maggie.

But Maggie was kind, compassionate, and generous—three things that were hard to come by in this city. She might redefine the word "quirky," and she might operate on the shadier side of the law once in a while, but she was also the woman who'd invited me into her home for Christmas after finding out I had no plans and hadn't celebrated a holiday in years.

Even if I hadn't had an alternate plan from the start, I wouldn't have delivered her into the world of holding cells and gray jumpsuits that had entrapped me.

Leaning closer, I whispered, "I'm going to show you something, and I need you to stay calm."

She nodded nervously. I gave her a hard look, ensuring she was prepared.

Then I let the café hallucination die.

12

MAGGIE'S EYES WIDENED as the vision of a cozy, kitschy café faded to reveal the cold, modern reality. With so much mental space freed, I redirected my focus to where I needed it far more.

Sucking in a sharp breath, she pressed her hands to the table as though to stand.

"Don't react," I hissed urgently. "We're being watched."

She settled back into her seat. "What's going on? What did you do?"

"Don't look, but did you notice those two tense-looking people in the corner?"

"Yes, yes. Who are they?"

"MPD agents."

Fear washed over Maggie's face. "What? Why? Are you working for the MPD?"

"I'm just trying to survive."

"We're all trying to survive," she countered angrily. "Don't forget that. We're all trying to keep our heads above water."

I squashed my guilt down. "I didn't get away, Maggie. They caught me, and they've got sixty-one charges piled on my head."

"So you're throwing me to the wolves to save yourself?"

"Not even close," I growled. "You told me once that an anti-telethesian potion is a staple in your emergency kit. Please tell me you have that with you."

"Is one of those agents a telethesian?" She shook her head sharply. "Of course I have a potion, but evading them won't work when they're watching."

My hand clenched around the necklace. "I'll handle that part for us."

"Us?"

"I'm coming with you."

Her eyes widened, then she nodded.

"Go to the restroom and stay there until I call you. Have that potion ready."

She gave me a twitchy, humorless smile, then pushed back from the table. Lienna and Agent Cutter tensed, then relaxed again when she headed for the ladies' room. They already knew there was no way out of the building from that direction.

My heart drummed a nervous beat against my ribs.

There are three basic hallucination tricks I've mastered. The Redecorator was the first one—altering bits and pieces of a space to suit my needs. One of my favorite pranks growing up was targeting a classroom bully or asshole foster parent and moving a curb or a chair a few inches. I can't tell you how many sprained ankles and bruised butts I'm personally responsible for.

People, however, have a *presence* in the minds of others in a way that white paint and a gumball machine don't. Changing the color of someone's sweater, sure, no problem. But creating a hallucination of a person speaking, moving, or emoting differently while the real deal is in plain view? The human brain resists hard when I try anything like that.

Which was why I needed the real Maggie out of sight before attempting this next part.

I counted to one hundred in my head, then concentrated on the Maggie I knew—which, by the way, was a big help. Knowing her, I mean. Made the hallucination way more convincing.

The bathroom door swung open and Maggie walked out with that same nervous skitter, her attention darting around as it had when she'd entered the café. She walked to our table and stopped beside her chair, fidgeting with a snap on her overalls.

Or so it appeared.

Now for the even harder part.

I stood up from my chair, bent my head toward Maggie, and whispered to her. She nodded, then marched for the door.

Agent Cutter and Lienna lurched to their feet, and I canted my head toward them, giving a quick thumbs-up and a "follow me" gesture. All part of the plan, my smile said.

Lienna lifted the chain of her necklace enough to peer at the cat's eye. Reassured that her anti-psychic spell was in place, she waited as I joined Maggie at the exit. After the door swung shut behind us, the two agents rushed into motion, hurrying out onto the sidewalk in stealthy pursuit.

I watched them go, still sitting in my chair.

Creating a fake-Maggie wouldn't work if she was in view because I couldn't completely disguise the real version. But that limitation? It doesn't apply to *me*. Faking myself—or even erasing myself—was a piece of halluci-cake.

Keeping my gaze trained out the window, I navigated the vision of me and Maggie across the street and into a busy all-you-can-eat sushi joint. Like the good trackers they were, Lienna and Agent Cutter followed.

The moment they disappeared inside, I dropped the hallucination and yelled, "Maggie!"

The handful of customers and the barista jumped in surprise, but I didn't care. We had no time to waste.

Maggie burst out of the bathroom, her cell phone in one hand and a small vial in the other. As she rushed toward me, I shoved up from my seat and tossed the necklace down.

The cat's eye clattered against the tabletop.

How long before Lienna realized the necklace she wore was the shark-tooth pendant? How long before she realized I'd switched them, and all this time I'd been projecting a vision of the cat's eye pendant into her brain? She'd thought she was safe from my ability, but I'd had her mind in my hold since the moment she removed the protective spell from around her neck.

Slapping her phone down, a text message conversation open on the screen, Maggie yanked the stopper out of the vial and took a sip of the contents, then passed it to me.

I poured the second dose into my mouth. Bitter onion bloomed over my tongue. Yuck.

"It'll only last a few minutes," she warned.

I grabbed her hand. "Then let's go!"

We bolted across the dining floor and behind the counter. Ignoring the barista's angry protest, I hauled Maggie through the back room and out the rear door. We rushed into a damp alley.

Were Lienna and Agent Cutter backtracking yet? If they returned to the café, the barista could point them in our direction.

As we sprinted down the alley, Maggie's phone rang, the sound bouncing off the surrounding buildings. She pressed it to her ear. "We're heading toward 12th Avenue. Can you be there in—yes, perfect!"

"Who was that?" I demanded as we cut left down a narrow street.

"I had someone waiting to pick me up."

Ah, Maggie. So paranoid. I loved it.

Drizzly rain clung to my hair and chilled the back of my neck as we jogged down several more streets and into another alley. Ahead, I could see the corner of 12th. Almost there. Almost safe.

As we raced for the corner, a beat-up sedan the color of a bad sunburn pulled across the alley opening, blocking it. The passenger door swung wide, the driver reaching across the seat to open it, his face in shadow.

A beaming smile of relief spread across Maggie's face, and she sprinted ahead of me. As I scrambled to follow, my own relief lightened my body. Yes! I was escaping! The moment I got in that car, I'd be home free.

"Hi, baby," Maggie gushed breathlessly, sliding onto the seat.

Baby? She had a *baby*? Since when? A weirdly affectionate, bubbly happiness spread through my chest, competing with the cold suspicion that was overtaking my relief.

I'd been heading for the car's back door, but instead, I veered toward the passenger door. Maggie grabbed the handle to swing it shut in my face. I caught the edge and shoved it back open. Bending down, I looked across her to the driver.

The man smiled in a friendly way. "Hey, Kit."

My mouth hung open. I knew that blond-haired, blue-eyed Garrett Hedlund lookalike.

"Quentin?" I blurted.

"*Quentin*," Maggie cooed, leaning across the center console to nuzzle his shoulder with her face. "I missed you."

"Missed you too, Mags."

I was … *so* … confused.

The empath wrapped his arm around her waist as he studied me. "Maggie said you're working with the MPD and you set her up. That true, Kit?"

She hadn't wasted any time filling him in while I lured Lienna and Agent Cutter away, had she?

"I wasn't setting her up," I told him tersely. "I was *escaping*, just like you did. I want to come with you."

I wasn't sure I wanted to join in on whatever the hell they had going on, but I needed to get in that car. Lienna and Agent Cutter were probably searching for my trail. I had minutes at best, seconds at worst, to disappear.

Quentin arched his eyebrows. "We don't got room in here for traitors."

"I'm a traitor? What about *you*? You sent Jeff and Geoff after me!" I wasn't sure why that was relevant to the conversation. I could have countered with something about how I'd only cooperated as a way to escape, but I was too distracted by the way Maggie was half crawling into Quentin's lap while cooing affectionately—and the unsettling urge I had to do the same thing.

"I sent them after any MagiPol assholes who were following me. Not my fault you switched sides." He shook his head. "How long have you been their bitch, Kit?"

"I'm still on your side, Quentin. I just needed to get away. Now I'm away."

"Too late, man. Me and Mags were gonna invite you in on our plans, but I'm not risking everything for a rat."

He reached across Maggie and grabbed the door handle. I tightened my grip on the top of the door, opening my mouth to argue.

"Bye-bye, Kit."

His blue eyes fixed on me—and a potent blast of fear weakened my legs. As I staggered backward, he yanked the door from my grasp. It slammed shut. The engine revved, then the car pulled away. It zoomed into the misty rain.

I stared after them, the cold drizzle soaking my hair.

That was it. The two people who were the closest semblances to friends I had in Vancouver had left me on the curb like a heap of useless trash.

13

AS I STOOD THERE in a pathetic stupor, the obnoxious squeal of air brakes pierced my ears. Twenty yards down the street, a city bus had pulled up at a stop. The doors creaked open and a pair of women in business slacks got off while an old lady with an umbrella and a cane waited to board.

Maggie's anti-telethesian potion had probably expired by now, and this neighborhood would be crawling with agents in a matter of minutes.

I bolted down the sidewalk. The slow granny had inched onto the bus, and I jumped in after her. She tapped her bus pass on the card reader next to the driver and it flashed green.

I, of course, was sans wallet. My bus pass was in the care of the MPD, along with my credit cards, driver's license, and a Starbucks gift card worth a whopping ten bucks.

Focusing on the bus driver, I stuck my arm out. The bus pass hallucination in my real hand tapped the reader, and I added an approving green light before shuffling toward the back of the bus. As I sank onto a seat across from the rear door, the bus accelerated away from the café.

Breathing slow and deep, I closed my eyes.

It hadn't gone to plan, but I'd done it. I'd escaped.

Well, sort of. There was the telethesian problem. All Agent Cutter had to do was find my trail at the bus stop and he could, in theory, track me forever. Imagine a predator—a bearded, plaid-adorned, axe-wielding predator—who could always find you. It was the ultimate "you can run, but you can't hide" situation.

It was almost as scary as the *Predator* predator.

I knew a few methods to slow down or throw off a telethesian, but they weren't all that convenient. My best shot was sticking to vehicular travel. Though it wouldn't obscure my psychic trail, it would hamper Agent Cutter's tracking progress.

The bus took me into the downtown core where I switched to another. After a few blocks, I got off and grabbed another one headed in a different direction, each time using my bus pass hallucination to board.

One more bus change and I found myself heading into a coastal suburb called Deep Cove that had a sleepy, Hallmark vibe to it. The sun had set and the streets were quiet.

Not good. Not good at all.

Don't get me wrong; I desperately wanted to buy an artisanal donut, get some organic kombucha, and book a week-long stay at a cozy bed and breakfast. But if I rounded up all the people I could see on the street, I wouldn't be able to field an entire baseball team, and that was a problem, because mixing in with a crowd was another way to muddy a telethesian's tracking.

But taking this bus back into the crowded downtown core, where Lienna, Agent Cutter, and any number of other agents would be tracking my wacky bus trail, wasn't smart either.

The thought of Lienna desperately chasing me across the Greater Vancouver area set off a pang of guilt in my gut that hit much harder than I'd expected. I didn't want to think about her reaction when she realized I'd tricked her—her shock, disappointment, shame, and vindicated loathing for the traitorous, untrustworthy crook. She'd vouched for me. She'd offered to take care of my most precious belongings. She'd given me an evening out of my jail cell, and it'd been the most pleasant night I'd had in recent memory—even before my arrest.

On top of the emotional slap to the face I'd given her, Captain Blythe wasn't the forgiving type. When Lienna returned to the precinct without me, Blythe could and probably would extract a career-destroying punishment from the rookie agent.

I clenched my jaw. Guilt pangs or not, neither Lienna's feelings nor her career ranked as high on my priority list as my life.

Standing, I pressed the "next stop" button on the pole beside my seat. The bus doors opened, and I hopped onto the sidewalk. I wasn't sure what time it was—I didn't have a watch or a phone—but my best guess was after ten p.m., which meant most businesses were closed.

Choosing a random direction, I started walking. As I rounded a corner, the sidewalk declined steeply toward the town center: a cutesy row of coffee shops and clothing boutiques. All closed. Apparently, Deep Cove wasn't a "lively nightlife" sort of place.

Near the end of the street was a small hotel with a French restaurant on the first floor. Behind the hotel, a pier stuck out into the town's eponymous cove, and a couple dozen boats were docked alongside it.

Jackpot.

The best way to elude a telethesian: water. Taking a long shower wouldn't hide me from Agent Jack Cutter, but taking a boat out onto the ocean would sever my trail. It was the only sure-fire way to escape those pesky, mythical bloodhounds—well, aside from jumping on an airplane, but I didn't have any of *those* handy.

I entered the hotel lobby, painted almost entirely in a pastel blue color. To match the ocean, I guess. The receptionist, a guy in his mid-thirties with spiky, bleach-blond hair and bags under his crazed-looking eyes, greeted me.

"Hey, man!" he said with jittery excitement. "How can I help you?"

"I'm just looking for a restroom."

The receptionist nodded with the same vigor as a mechanical paint shaker. "Yeah, man. We definitely have one of those."

He snatched up an energy drink from behind the counter, downed the whole thing, crushed the can in his fist, and tossed it over his shoulder. Holy balls. This guy was so damn caffeinated his heartbeat probably sounded like a hummingbird's.

"Bathroom?" I prompted.

"Right! Right, right, right." He twisted his arm to point down a hallway. "Head on down there, man. Third door on your right. No, fourth." He twitched a bit. "No, third."

"I'll figure it out."

Sure enough, three doors down on the right was the men's bathroom. Inside, I headed straight to the garbage can—one of those metal ones built directly into the wall. Lucky for me, it had a bag in it.

I carefully removed the black plastic bag, doing my best not to rip it, then dumped its contents back into the empty bin and turned it inside out. After picking all the tissues and gum off the bag, I crumpled it up, jammed it in my jacket pocket, and washed my hands.

I gave the chemical-powered receptionist a quick wave as I exited the hotel. Outside, I opted to head around the rear of the building instead of returning to the street. The more twists and turns I could take, the better. I passed through a small community playground—crossing the monkey bars like a pro, just for good measure—and headed down toward the marina. Keeping my ears alert for a raging smart car engine, I approached a big barred gate with a "Yacht Club" sign on it.

What did they do in a Yacht Club, exactly? Pondering the possibilities—Yacht-based mock sea battles? If so, sign me up— I scaled the gate and dropped down on the other side. The marina appeared abandoned, and if anyone spotted me, well, I wasn't too worried.

I ambled down the pier, checking left and right. Sailing a yacht was well outside my skill set, but just maybe … aha!

Moored in a corner and bumping against a post with each ripple of water was a little tin can of a boat, probably used to grab shit people dropped in the ocean or something. A small outboard motor was attached to the back, but more importantly, a pair of wooden oars lay in the bottom.

I climbed down, wrangled the mooring rope free, and shoved away from the pier. Grabbing the oars, I got in position.

"Row, row, row your boat, heading straight to sea," I sang under my breath as the oars dipped into the dark water. "Merrily, merrily, merrily, merrily, escape the MPD."

Ten minutes later, I was breathing hard and my arms were burning in a nice, "good workout" kind of way. That would soon deteriorate to a "this is hell" kind of burn, but I'd enjoy it while it lasted.

The lights of Deep Cove shrank, then disappeared as I laboriously rowed my way out of the cove and into the inlet. It was hella dark out on the water, the cool wind nipping at my face and aching in my ears. Picking out the coastline, I followed it south.

When I could no longer make out any lights on my right, I angled the boat toward the coast. Pulling the oars in, I tugged the hotel garbage bag from my pocket. Then I stripped naked.

Yeah, completely naked. I took every shred of clothing I had on, bundled it up into the garbage bag, then tied it around my wrist, ensuring it was sealed tight. With a deep breath, I positioned myself at the edge of the boat.

I really wished this wasn't necessary, but I wasn't bringing any boat evidence to shore. Teeth clenched, I jumped overboard.

Holy sweet yeti on an icicle cracker! Cold! So very, very cold!

Icy water engulfed my head, and I popped back to the surface, feet kicking. My teeth were already chattering and my lungs had contracted to a quarter their normal size. It might have been early June, but nighttime ocean water in the Pacific Northwest could never be mistaken for warm.

Wondering if I'd lost my goddamn mind, I glanced back at the boat, but my enthusiastic leap had pushed it away, and it was drifting farther while I treaded water.

Well, nothing to do but swim.

I pushed into a one-armed breaststroke, doing my damnedest to keep my head and clothing bag above the salty ocean water. The feeling in my hands and feet had vanished and my motor skills were rapidly diminishing, but I powered toward the dark shore. Not that far.

I squinted ahead. Actually, it was a good bit farther than I'd intended. Shit.

Don't think about sharks, I told myself. Don't think about the creature from the black lagoon. Don't think about frostbitten genitalia or what the newspaper headlines will say when they find my frozen, fully nude cadaver, half-eaten by fish, washed up on the shore of Japan with a garbage bag full of clothes tied to my wrist.

Think positive. This wasn't even the coldest I'd ever been. Crazy, right?

When I was thirteen, Douchebag Dwayne, the worst foster parent of all time, took me to basketball practice at my junior high school. He insisted I play, not because I was good or he had any love for the game, but because the other parents were perfect customers for the illegal lottery tickets he was selling.

While Dwayne tried to auction off scratch-and-wins, I pocketed the cash I'd stolen from his wallet, snuck out the back door, and took off into the night. Two problems immediately arose: my internal GPS failing me, and Dwayne failing to provide his foster son with a winter coat despite Canadian winters averaging roughly a billion degrees below zero.

So I ended up lost in a blizzard for over an hour without a proper jacket.

As I kicked my bare legs in the hypothermic water, I hoped this freezing cold experience turned out better. My thirteen-year-old self *did* survive. I even made it to the bus station, but the ticket kiosk lady pegged me for a runaway and, instead of selling me a ticket, called the cops.

I ended up right back where I began: in a bedroom with three other foster kids, wishing I was free. Thanks, kiosk lady.

My arm caught on a frond of slimy seaweed and I cringed. Kicking harder, I sliced a path through the marine vegetation. When my hand contacted another surface, it was the rocky bottom. Thank god.

I got my legs under me, only to realize my feet were entirely numb. After a few missteps, I waded out of the water and collapsed on a grassy patch at the tree line, puffing for air through violent shivers. My fingers were so frozen that untying the garbage bag from my wrist was impossible. I ripped it open and yanked out my clothes, which were, by some miracle, still dry.

Once I was dressed and my extremities had begun to warm up, pins and needles assaulted my nerves. I balled my hands into fists and shook my legs out, trying to drive the blood back into my veins, all the while gauging the surrounding landscape.

I was at the bottom of a hill, which was just awesome. A good ol' uphill stroll was exactly what I needed right now. Ugh.

Once the burning sensation in my feet subsided, I started my trek toward civilization. Back toward the city and crowds of people and, undoubtedly, back toward danger. But also, I hoped, toward freedom.

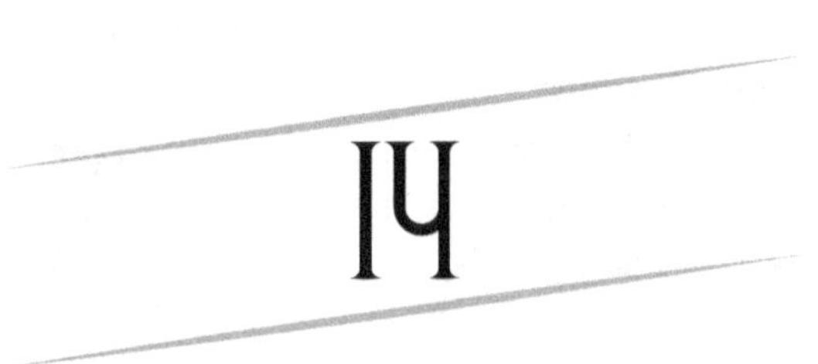

WHEN I STUMBLED into the twenty-four-hour convenience store, soaking wet and shivering, the eighteen-year-old behind the counter would've been on the phone to the cops in an instant—if that's what I'd let him see.

Instead of the trembling, hunched-over mess that I was, I showed the clerk an upright and thoroughly dry version of myself. The hallucination Kit smiled in greeting and ambled into the beef jerky section.

Meanwhile, I stood just inside the door, rubbing my hands together and dripping water on the floor. After all that effort to keep my clothes dry, it'd started pouring rain three minutes after my exit from the ocean. Mother Nature had a cruel sense of humor.

My ribs felt like they were covered in frost, but I didn't let that interfere with the hallucination I was projecting into the clerk's mind. While I remained invisible, my doppelganger somberly debated between Butter Mesquite and Chicago Smoke jerky, his head bobbing back and forth.

I could thank Douchebag Dwayne for my mastery of this skill, which I'd affectionately dubbed Split Kit. It'd started out as a trick in school—fooling my teachers into thinking I was paying attention while I doodled or read a book. It wasn't until I met Dwayne and his swinging fists that I learned to make myself entirely invisible.

As I sent fake-Kit toward the candy aisle, I tiptoed around the counter to join the clerk. His cell phone sat beside the register, and I made the device invisible as I palmed it. I prodded the screen. No passcode. Perfect.

Retreating to the corner, I sent fake-Kit in the opposite direction—though not toward the cooler doors with their shiny glass. Reflections were way too tricky to pull off while distracted.

Dialing the number I'd memorized three days ago, I lifted the phone to my ear. It rang. And rang … and rang and rang. Finally, it went to voicemail, and my heart sank.

"Jenkins, it's Kit," I murmured in a low tone so my voice wouldn't carry to the clerk. "I escaped. I'm at a convenience store south of Deep Cove. On Dollarton Highway, I think. If you can find me, I could use your help."

As I disconnected the call, I realized the clerk was squinting at fake-Kit in confusion. Shit on a stick. I was losing my grip on the hallucination and its uncanniness was coming through.

Hurrying into the nearest aisle, I stuffed my pockets full of Slim Jims, Sour Patch Kids, and a couple bottles of water. Meanwhile, fake-Kit approached the clerk.

"Hey," he asked casually, "do you know where the nearest hotel is?"

The clerk frowned. "The closest one is by the cove. Or back toward town. I think there's one by Capilano."

"Nothing closer?"

"Nah, man."

Damn it. I couldn't go back to Deep Cove because there was an excellent chance that Lienna and Agent Cutter were hunting for me in that area. Capilano was a long way away.

Fake-Kit wished him a good night, then we both exited and coalesced into a single entity.

Pulling my hood over my head against the steady rain, I crossed the parking lot back toward the sidewalk. If Jenkins came through for me, this was where he'd show up, so I didn't want to go far.

Half a block down the street, a bus stop with a glass-walled shelter posed under a yellow streetlight. Good enough. I hurried into the shelter and collapsed onto the bench, rain drumming against the metal roof. My shoulders, which had been squeezed up around my ears to keep out the chill, relaxed, and I tore into a Slim Jim.

In my other hand was the phone I'd stolen, and I stared at it, fighting the sick feeling in my gut. I'd called a virtual stranger for help … because there was no one else. Maggie and Quentin had been my only friends.

If I called Lienna and asked her to help me, what would she say?

I snorted quietly. She'd probably turn me into a legless poodle through the phone line out of pure rage. I'd betrayed her like the slimy crook she'd assumed I was from the very start.

Betrayed, though … that was a harsh word. Tricked, yes. Hung out to dry, sure. But betrayed? I rifled through my internal thesaurus for a better option. Before we'd almost died in Rigel's secret office, and before she'd taken me to my apartment and we'd watched a movie, and before she'd vouched for me in front of Blythe, I wouldn't have worried about the best descriptor for my actions. But now?

My stomach turned over, unhappy with the Slim Jim. Or maybe that squirmy feeling was guilt.

I didn't feel guilty for saving my own ass, though. Ditching unpleasant situations and vanishing into the night was my go-to survival move.

You're an orphan with no family to speak of, and the only people willing to take you in are abusive shit stains? Run away.

The foster system can't figure out what to do with you because, unbeknownst to everyone—including you—you're a freaky mythic and you weird everyone out? Run away.

The law firm you work for turns out to be run by money-grubbing conmen and collapses? Definitely run away.

Some people might call it cowardly, but I call it self-preservation. And it'd never bothered me before. Maybe I'd trampled over Lienna's burgeoning trust and small kindnesses on my way to freedom, but what else could I have done? Waited to see if the MPD would execute me?

Determinedly munching on my ill-gotten snacks, I turned my thoughts toward a topic that didn't make my gut twitch. Like Maggie's strange behavior. And Quentin's asshole behavior—not that Quentin being an asshole was a surprise.

Yeah, he'd always been self-centered, but calling *me* a traitor when he'd revealed my existence to the MPD? Total bullshit. If not for him, I would've caught that flight and vanished somewhere in the South Pacific long before the MPD learned about "that intern guy who never shuts up about movies."

The behavior of Quentin's new "baby" was way weirder. Greed-condemning, paranoid Maggie was aiding and abetting a fugitive? Helping with his Blue-Smoke-related plans? Endangering herself for profit?

All wrong.

While it was totally Quentin's MO to manipulate people, he had a particular type when it came to women, and Maggie was about ten years too old and five hundred percent too quirky for him. Obviously, he was using his empath abilities to make her think she loved him. I mean, even *I'd* felt like snuggling up on his lap, and last I checked, I didn't bat for that team. His gooey love waves had caught me when I got too close.

I slumped back against the glass wall. Quentin would only be influencing Maggie if he needed something from her, and the only thing he desired right now was Blue Smoke. Rigel had wanted Maggie's help to break into Cerberus. If Quentin had taken over the heist plan, he must want her help too. And unlike Rigel, he wasn't giving Maggie the option to refuse.

Though Quentin was manipulating her on a level that surpassed "mean" and delved straight to "traumatizing evil," there was nothing I could do about it. I was no match for Quentin, and even if I were, I had no idea where he'd taken Maggie or how to find them or … anything. Besides, I had my own survival to worry about.

Despite that, a new dollop of cold guilt joined the weight that had settled deep in my gut.

I finished a bag of candy, threw it in the garbage can next to the bus stop, and dropped back onto the bench. Exhaustion filtered through me—mental and physical. Redecorating the café for Maggie while altering the necklace for Lienna, then all sorts of Split Kit shenanigans during my escape … I was beat.

My eyelids were drooping when something across the street caught my attention: a person standing at the edge of the curb, watching me. Tall, lean, dressed in dark clothes. Shadows masked the details of their face.

They didn't have the stick-up-the-ass rigor of an MPD agent, but they *did* have the leather-clad intensity of a bounty hunter.

Lienna hadn't wasted any goddamn time, had she? The moment I'd escaped, she'd probably pushed my name, mug shot, and villainous description to every mythic guild in the city. I wondered how big a bounty Blythe had authorized. How bad did she want my handsome face back in her interrogation room?

The figure across the street stepped off the curb and walked toward me.

I sprang off the bench, accidentally dropping the stolen phone. I needed to get out of there—but I didn't know what I was dealing with. A sorcerer? A telekinetic? A mage? I had to find out.

Time for my third, and arguably coolest, hallucination power: Creature Feature. I didn't get to use this one often because it lacked the subtlety of Split Kit and the Redecorator. Surprisingly, terrifying people wasn't that useful in day-to-day life.

I imagined a big-ass monster truck with blinding headlights and screaming wheels. Then I projected the image of that truck, blasting down the road, onto the person approaching me.

In theory, a roaring monster truck about to flatten you into the pavement should garner a reaction: you jump out of the way, or reveal your magic to deflect the truck, or scream and leave a new brown stain in your underpants.

In reality, the approaching mythic gave a slight flinch, then kept walking.

What. The. Shit.

Okay, well, time to run for it. I turned on my heel and bolted—and the bounty hunter sprinted after me, angling to cut me off.

Excellent. They were fearless *and* they had the reaction time of a genetically mutated ninja cat.

My survival drive fueled my legs, and I kicked it up another notch, running so fast the rain didn't seem to touch me. Unfortunately, the ninja cat was also pretty damn quick.

"Kit!" they yelled. "Stop!"

Oh yeah, sure. Just because you asked so nicely.

As I dashed down the sidewalk, I concentrated. Split Kit veered left across the road—and I, now invisible to my pursuer, careened to the right.

The bounty hunter took the bait. Praise be to Ralph Ellison. Slowing to a jog as I ascended a grassy hill toward a set of warehouses, I sent fake-Kit into the trees on the road's other side. Ninja-cat zoomed after him in hot pursuit—then threw on the brakes.

They skidded to a halt. Paused. Then whipped around and ran back across the road—right toward me. How? I was *invisible!*

"Stop, Kit!" they called. "I'm not gonna hurt you!"

Like I was going to take their word for it.

Up ahead, a seven-foot fence made of corrugated metal panels ran alongside the closest warehouse. Rousing all the adrenaline and athleticism I had within me, I leaped at the fence, grabbed the top edge, and pulled myself over with relative dexterity.

The second I hit the ground on the other side, I took off in between the building and the fence. At the first intersection of buildings, I wheeled left. Then right. Right again, then left. Even if the bounty hunter could see through my hallucinations, they couldn't see through walls. Unless they were a telethesian, in which case I was screwed. I tried not to think about that.

I whipped around another corner and came face to face with a locked gate. Breathing hard, I scrambled over it with significantly less nimbleness and landed on the other side.

And there they were: the ninja cat, waiting for me.

As it turned out, the bounty hunter was a leather-clad woman in her twenties with short blond hair shaved on the sides and the air of a gangster who could barehandedly rip my head from my shoulders. In her knee-high boots, she was nearly the same height as me.

She raised her hands as though approaching a wild animal in a trap.

Geez. Lienna must have put some nasty-sounding shit on the MPD's online bounty board: "Unarmed and extremely annoying. His hallucinations are worse than his bite. Deal with him like you would a feral kitten."

The bounty hunter opened her mouth to say something, but I wasn't all that interested in a chat, so I split myself once more, sending fake-Kit to the right while invisi-Kit dove to the left.

Before I could take a full step, she snapped her leg out. The kick slammed into my gut, throwing me off balance, and unable to stop my momentum, I pitched sideways.

I didn't even see what stupid warehouse junk I fell into, but my head cracked against something wretchedly hard and my vision went black.

MY ENTIRE EXISTENCE was swaying, gently rocking back and forth like a baby in a cradle. A baby with a massive headache.

I let out a long groan as my eyes fluttered open. A cramped, dimly lit room with a low ceiling and wood-paneled walls came into focus, and it took me a moment to realize I was horizontal—sprawled out on a small bed tucked against one wall. And I wasn't imagining that everything was swaying.

Where the hell was I? Wincing, I gingerly touched the side of my head where I'd cracked my skull on something.

A woman's voice broke through the darkness. "Don't freak out, okay?"

The lightning-reflexed bounty hunter walked into the light, holding a glass of water in one hand and a bottle of pills in the other. I scrambled into a sitting position, and the pounding in my head immediately made me regret that decision.

"I told you not to freak out. You're kinda spazzy, aren't ya?" She tossed the bottle of pills at me. "Take a couple of those."

"What are they? Poison? Truth serum?"

"Advil, dummy. For your head."

I fished the bottle out of the blankets. Extra-strength Advil. "You could've tampered with them."

"I'm not an alchemist, dude." The leather-clad lady set the glass of water on a small table beside me, then sat on a folding chair. "Take them. Or don't. I honestly don't give a shit."

I opened the bottle and peeked inside. Looked like Advil, smelled like Advil. "Where are we?"

"On my boat."

That explained the swaying. "Why are we on your boat?"

"Because I didn't wanna be hanging out with your unconscious ass in the middle of nowhere when the MPD showed up."

Wait, what? Avoiding the MPD meant avoiding her paycheck for tagging me. Unless … "You aren't a bounty hunter?"

"Hell no. I'm not doing the MPD's dirty work for them. I'm a smuggler. Basically the opposite of a bounty hunter."

All that running and projecting and skull cracking for nothing. She hadn't shown up to capture me; she'd shown up to rescue me. "Did Jenkins send you?"

"Yeah. He knows I dock my boat close to Deep Cove, so he sent me after you when he got your message."

In light of this new information, Advil suddenly seemed like a fantastic idea. I popped a couple in my mouth and washed them down with the water she'd left me, praying the dose would kick in soon.

Closing my eyes against the outrageous throbbing in my head, I mumbled, "So … who are you?"

"Vera."

"I'm Kit."

"I know."

"Right." I pressed a hand to my bruised gut. "You've got a mean roundhouse, Vera."

"Yeah, sorry about that." She didn't sound sorry at all. "I kinda panicked when you tried to run again."

"And your first reaction was to kick my kidney through my spine?"

She gave a small laugh. "People say violence doesn't solve anything, but I find it solves a whole helluva lot." A pause. "So you assumed I was a bounty hunter working for the MPD?"

"Yeah."

"Hm. Cool monster truck, by the way."

I didn't need to open my eyes to pick up on her faint sarcasm. "Thanks."

"Did you make up the flames on the sides and everything?" Her joking condescension grew more palpable.

"No, I had a toy that looked like that."

"Cute. So, you're an illusionist?"

"It's more like a hallucination."

"Meaning I was the only one who saw your super-rad monster truck?" she asked, continuing her playful derision.

"Yeah."

She went silent, so I opened my eyes to find her zoned out. Her gaze was focused on something distant, which was odd because nothing in this tiny room could be considered distant. Was she having a seizure?

"Are you okay?"

She blinked a couple of times and her eyes refocused. "Sorry, what?"

"What were you doing?"

"Seeing."

"Seeing … what?"

"The future. I'm a seer."

Ohhh. That explained a lot. Seers, as Rigel had once longingly explained, could see several seconds to several minutes into the future. That might not sound like a lot, but a twenty-second heads-up could save your life in a whole lot of sticky situations.

It also explained how she'd known my monster truck wouldn't smoosh her, and where I would run. Split Kit wasn't so useful if she could foresee that my duplicate would disappear.

"What did you see?" I asked warily.

"Nothing interesting, which means we don't have to worry about unwanted guests. Not for the next five minutes, at least," she added. "I'm guessing you're not hoping for a reunion with the MPD anytime soon."

That was a safe assumption. I got more comfortable on the bed, my damp clothes squishing unpleasantly. "How do you know Jenkins?"

"We're in the same guild. He kicks the odd client over to me and I give him a cut if it turns into anything."

"You have clients?"

"What do you think you are?" She noticed my hesitation. "That's what you need, isn't it? Someone to help you get the hell out of here?"

"Uh, yeah." And I'd already pieced together how the next part of our conversation would go. If Jenkins was getting a cut, that meant Vera expected payment for helping me—which was a problem, because even if I'd had my wallet, the contents of my bank account now belonged to the MPD.

She sighed. "You don't have any money, do you?"

"I'm a fugitive on the run. What did you expect?"

"I don't do charity work."

"Not even for fellow MPD-hating mythics on the run and in dire need of assistance?"

She crossed her arms. Looked like a "no."

"Maybe we can work something out?" I was grasping at straws, but if Vera bailed on me, I was back at square zero without a dry pair of underwear to my name. "I'm sure we can come to an arrangement. *Quid pro quo.* You know."

"*Quid pro quo?*"

"It means—"

"I know what it means. What can you offer me?"

"What do you need?" I asked, sounding exponentially more confident than I felt. "Maybe I can hook you up with a shiny new hallucination, and in return, you can ship me a long way away from here."

Her lips pursed thoughtfully, and I tried not to look too hopeful. I would give her an entire bucketful of projections, hallucinations, and whatever else I could conjure up if it got me out of this mess. It's not like it would cost me anything to dream up an imaginary dragon.

"All that dual shit you pulled when you were running was kinda impressive." She eyed me. "I bet you've got a lot of those tricks up your sleeve."

"Oh yeah, tons of them. Up my very wet sleeve. You saw the monster truck."

"A glorified Hot Wheels toy?" she scoffed. "You can do better than that."

Going after my pride, was she? A good tactic, but I didn't let her aggravate me. "I could put you in the middle of a monster truck jam right now, if that's what you're looking for. The whole deal. You know, the 'Sunday, Sunday, Sunday, you pay for the whole seat, but you'll only need the edge' type thing."

Creating a full-fledged hallucination with no basis in reality, set in a dreamed-up location with moving pieces and sound, was a tall order. Too tall for me. But I wasn't going to tell her that.

"I might have something you can help me with," she mused, "if you're willing to do what I ask."

"And what is that?"

"You're gonna help me rob an artifact dealer."

I squinted, wondering if I'd misheard. She'd said the words as though they were no big deal. "Say what now?"

"He stole from me first," she proclaimed defensively. "He set me up with a client—some white-collar windbag who cheated his guild and needed to run. I wasn't super hyped about helping a jackass like that, but he was gonna pay real well. Everything went smoothly. I dropped him off and he waved goodbye and we both sailed off into the sunset. Then a couple hours later, I'm looking for an enchanted watch I got as payment from another client and it's gone—along with the rest of my stash. The bastard took it all."

"And you think this artifact dealer put him up to it?" I asked.

"I *know* it."

"How?"

"I'm in the smuggling business, Kit. Word gets around. He's about to run a nice little auction, and half the items on the menu are my artifacts."

"Are they valuable?"

"They're my life savings." She grimaced. "I need some air."

Abandoning her seat, she climbed the narrow half-ladder, half-staircase beside the kitchenette and ducked through a short door. The cool night breeze slipped inside, bringing with it the quiet lapping of waves, then the door clacked shut.

Maybe fresh air would be good for me too. I grabbed my shoes and followed her up onto the deck.

The clouds had cleared, revealing a masterpiece of twinkling stars. The dark water was calm, and the unexpected beauty of a quiet night was a welcome change from the life or death pace of the past few days.

Vera's boat was anchored to a short wooden dock in a small inlet around the curve of Deep Cove. The boat was, aside from a plentiful array of rust spots, mostly white and looked like it had seen a lot of time out on the open sea. Twenty feet long, it featured a covered platform that sat on top of the living quarters, which I assumed was where all the steering and captaining and serious boating took place.

A narrow set of stairs wound away from the dock, up the rocky cliff, and toward an excessively expensive home overlooking the water. I traced the pathway with my eyes, then glanced at Vera. "Is that your house too?"

"I just rent the dock from the homeowners. I think they own a bank or an investment firm or some shit like that."

I pushed my feet into my shoes, not bothering with the laces. Hopefully I wouldn't be running anytime soon. "How come you haven't gone to get your stuff back from this dealer yourself?"

"Are you kidding?" She gave me a disbelieving side-eye. "Ever heard of Faustus Trivium?"

Faustus Trivium? That was an amazing name I would have absolutely remembered if I'd ever heard it before. "Nope. Who is he?"

She sat on the edge of the boat, facing me. "He has a gang of shady mythics who hang around him, and he deals a lot of illegal artifacts to a lot of illegal people."

"And you want to send *me* in after him?"

"Oh, relax," she scoffed. "I'd go with you. And with that magic of yours, I'm sure we'd be just fine."

A sudden rock of the boat threw me off balance, and I damn near did the splits as my feet slid in opposite directions.

She snorted. "Watch your step, landlubber."

"It's slippery."

"This sale Faustus is putting on, hocking my shit." She tapped her fingers on her knee. "It's Thursday evening."

"What day is it today? Er, tonight?"

"Very early on Tuesday."

I gave her a hard look. "In other words, we have approximately no time to get your stuff back."

Shaking my head, I retreated below deck, my arms wrapped around my middle for warmth. I could hardly remember what dry clothes felt like.

She followed me inside. "There's a shower if you want to use it, but the hot water heater busted."

A hot shower would've been an absolute savior. I'd never hated anything as much as I hated that water heater right now.

While I debated the unpleasantness of icing my body in cold water all over again versus trying to sleep with that grimy saltwater feeling all over my skin, Vera opened a cupboard and dug around inside. She tossed me a towel, then threw an armful of clothing my way.

I frowned. There was an awful lot of pink in her selection of garments.

"Get clean," she told me. "And throw your wet clothes on the stairs. I'll hang them outside to dry. Shout if you need anything else."

"I haven't agreed to help steal your stuff," I pointed out.

She raised a single blond eyebrow. "But you will."

With that, she headed back to the deck, leaving me to face the tiny, icy shower alone. Not that I wanted company.

I got the shower going, washed off in record time, and exited in a state of violent shivers. Within five minutes, I was dry, dressed, and lounging on the small cot wedged between the sink and the stairs. My new outfit consisted of hot pink fuzzy socks, silky black pajama pants that fit too snugly in the vital areas, and a baggy rose sweatshirt emblazoned with a glittery skeleton giving the finger.

No way Vera didn't have more gender-neutral clothes, but whatever. I was too tired to care. Though, thinking about it, I wouldn't have cared even while wide awake.

I leaned back against the pillow and closed my eyes. The door rattled as Vera came in, and I cracked an eye open just long enough to watch her enter the bathroom. Water ran as she brushed her teeth or washed her face or whatever women did to get ready for bed.

The gentle rocking of the boat lured me toward sleep. It'd been a long, tiring, dramatic day—from meeting Maggie in the café, to the unexpected encounter with Quentin, to my exhausting, hypothermic escape, to winding up on a refurbished fishing boat with a mercurial smuggler.

And I could only guess what tomorrow would bring.

16

 was a shithole.

Buried on the east end of town between an abandoned gas station and a pay-by-the-hour hotel with barred windows, Corky's Cuisine was little more than a sign, a door, and a window so grimy you couldn't see inside. And based on the odor of deep-fried trash that wafted out its back door, "cuisine" was a real stretch.

Vera and I spent Tuesday morning—the later part of the morning, after sleeping—scoping the place and debating a plan of attack. After far too much standing, pacing, and trying not to breathe the back-alley reek, we retreated to a better neighborhood and grabbed an outdoor table at an Indian restaurant.

As we waited for our food, our conversation drifted from infiltration strategies to how I'd ended up in my current fun situation. I ran through my unpleasantly immersive MPD experience, touching on Lienna, Captain Blythe, the lumberjack, and my cellmate Duncan. She'd heard of the latter—or at least, she'd heard of a hydromage murderer with a three-hundred-thousand-dollar bounty on his head and a habit of shriveling up humans like raisins.

"And they put *you* in a cell with him?" Vera asked, waiting for the waitress to get out of earshot after delivering our meals. She dug her fork into her curry. "I thought you were a conman."

"Barely even that. I just worked for conmen."

She tore off a hunk of naan bread and stirred it around in her bowl, soaking up the hot and spicy juices. "That's typical MPD bullshit right there."

I swallowed a helping of my much milder butter chicken. "What do you mean?"

"Throwing a harmless intern in with a bona fide serial killer? That's insane. You two shouldn't even be in the same building."

"They only have one building."

"Are you defending them?"

"God, no."

She wiped her mouth. Her food was so spicy that her breath made my eyes burn from across the table. "Those bastards are so caught up in their control and authoritarianism that they forget they're dealing with real people."

That sure sounded like certain people in the MPD, namely Captain Blythe. "I guess so."

"You guess so?" She guffawed. "I'd think someone who went through what you did would be harder on them."

"Well, I mean, some of them are just trying to keep the peace."

"Some of them? Like *Agent Shen*?" Vera gave me a scathing look. "Was she pretty? Did she smile at you all nice while manipulating you into helping arrest your friend?"

I scowled. "I suggested it, not her. The point was to get out of the precinct to escape."

The fact I'd started to like Lienna had nothing to do with anything.

"And my point is that Shen is no better than the rest of them. She just hides it better." Vera rammed another piece of naan bread in her mouth. "My dad used to deal with those MagiPol bastards for his job sometimes."

"Your dad?"

"He was a community management liaison before he retired."

That sounded … normal. Based on the tattoos and the leather and the overall attitude, I'd assumed Vera had grown up on the streets of some grungy metropolis where she had to hunt rats for her supper.

"It was his *job* to arbitrate between mythic communities and the MPD," she carried on, ramming her fork into her bowl, "and all they ever did was jerk him around. Because what could he even do, right? You can't fight the MPD. You either fall in line or you hide in the shadows."

"Is that what you're doing? Hiding?"

"As far as the MPD is concerned, I am a law-abiding mythic who dabbles in bounty hunting."

"Don't we need MagiPol, though?" I speared a piece of chicken with my fork. "I mean, what would happen without the MPD? It'd be chaos, wouldn't it? They're the only thing keeping the human world from knowing about us."

"So what?" She chewed another mouthful of curry-flavored lava. "Do you think we need the MPD to keep us safe from humans?"

My mind drifted to the number of ankles I'd broken by "redecorating" a street curb, and compared to most mythics, my power was harmless. "I was more thinking the other way around. They need to keep humans safe from us."

She scoffed. "You're sounding an awful lot like a goddamn agent. MagiPol's whole game is keeping magic under wraps."

"'Keep it secret; keep it safe,'" I quoted quietly.

"Yeah, Gandalf. Like that. The MPD doesn't give a flying shit about keeping humans safe. They barely even care about keeping mythics safe. All they care about is keeping *magic* safe. You wanna know why?"

"I have a feeling you'll tell me either way."

"Power." She pointed her fork at me in emphasis. "MagiPol has serious clout with all the world powers. Presidents and kings and shit. Their heaviest card is keeping magic from leaking out into the human world, because nobody in charge wants that. It would be a serious inversion of the system if all of a sudden the X-Men were running around out in the open."

"I appreciate the reference, but we're not mutants. Technically speaking."

"Regimes would be toppled in no time because mythics would rule the land. So, the MPD keeps us regular mythics from screwing up their systems, and in return, the human leaders do basically whatever the MPD wants."

I leaned back in my chair. "That's a bleak outlook."

"It's not an outlook, Kit. It's reality." She shrugged, then wiped her nose with a sniffle. I guess she wasn't immune to the million-degree curry after all. "The MPD won't last forever.

Instagram and selfies and surveillance cameras are gonna make it real hard for us to stay hidden indefinitely. It's a miracle the only humans blabbing about us are wingnut conspiracy theorists who think Kubrick faked the moon landing."

"How do you know he didn't?"

"Trust me, he didn't fake anything. He was a mythic, but he wasn't a fraud."

"Stanley Kubrick was a *mythic?*" I gasped. *Everyone* at KCQ had known I was a movie buff. How could they have universally failed to mention that one of the greatest film directors of all time had magical powers?

"Yeah. A telepath."

"That is so awesome."

From there, the conversation devolved into a debate about the greatest Kubrick films of all time (*A Clockwork Orange* versus *Dr. Strangelove*) and then into a debate about the greatest directors of all time (Scorsese versus Kurosawa) and then back to our plan for stealing from Faustus Trivium.

It took the better part of the afternoon, but we nailed down a strategy. The only problem was I didn't have the skills necessary for the very first step. That skill? Making Vera invisible to every person in Faustus's crappy diner.

The "every person" part wasn't an issue. Targeting a bunch of individual minds gets hella tricky, but I can easily dump the same vision on everyone around me—a grenade instead of a sniper rifle. Or as I prefer to call it, a halluci-bomb. While this method requires far less focus, it saps my psychic fuel like a gas-guzzling pickup truck racing uphill. Still, I could handle it for long enough to pull off our little heist.

The real problem was the invisibility portion. I can make objects invisible no problem, and I make myself invisible whenever I do a Split Kit diversion. But just as I couldn't make Maggie invisible to aid in our escape from the café, I couldn't make Vera invisible. It never worked for some reason.

Now I needed to figure it out.

I gave it my first serious attempt once we were back on Vera's boat. Targeting her mind, I tried to imitate the Split Kit hallucination, pushing beyond myself and onto her.

The result? A semi-transparent Kit and a wholly opaque Vera.

Two hours of headache-inducing effort got me no further than that. Vera ditched me to get more food, and sitting alone in the gently rocking boat, I rubbed my temples. I could make myself invisible. I could make inanimate stuff invisible. Why couldn't I make Vera invisible?

With no new ideas, I practiced making objects on the boat vanish. It wasn't difficult—I did it all the time with Redecorator hallucinations. What was the roadblock between Vera's saltshaker and Vera herself?

I tried bigger objects: the microwave, the bed, the chair. I even stepped out onto the dock and made the entire damn boat disappear. I was David freaking Copperfield.

Vera returned with the sushi—beef teriyaki for me, and salmon sashimi with more wasabi than was safe for the standard human to consume for her—but my practice hadn't helped. As we consumed our respective Japanese dishes, the best I could do was invisify—invisiblate?—Vera's food as she brought it to her mouth.

Turns out that was an annoying thing to do, and it earned me a solid punch to the shoulder.

Giving up, I chewed through a piece of beef and half listened to her threatening to toss me into the ocean if I invisified her food ever again. Not very creative, as far as threats went. What about shaving off my flesh? Transforming my eyeballs into pizza toppings? Sending my bones to another universe?

Damn, Lienna's threats had been fun. Scary, but fun.

An unpleasant twinge ran through my gut as my thoughts wandered to the MPD agent. Where was she now? Still searching for me, or had she focused on my far more dangerous empath ex-friend? Had Blythe taken her off the case after my escape? Would the captain cripple Lienna's career out of spiteful vengeance?

Sounded like something Blythe would do.

I speared a crispy broccoli tree with my fork. Maggie's information about Blue Smoke circled in my brain. Their plans to steal from Cerberus. The secret vault Maggie had helped them create to seal away their prize, once they got it. Quentin wanted that prize, no doubt about it. He was picking up the pieces Rigel had abandoned in death, and the empath was more than capable of making a run at Cerberus on his own—especially now that he'd empathically charmed Maggie into helping him.

Maybe I should tip off Lienna. If I could get word to her …

Wait. What was I thinking? I wasn't risking recapture for anything, especially not an MPD agent. Even if that agent was Lienna.

I forced my attention back to Vera, my dumbass brain making dumbass comparisons between the two women who'd knocked my life off course in very different ways. One tall and blond, the other dark-haired and slimly built, with personalities even more disparate than their physical appearances.

And as I thought about how each woman was far more than she appeared, it hit me.

Eyes widening, I really looked at Vera. This time, I didn't concentrate on making the tall blond sitting across from me invisible. I focused on *Vera*—her whole presence. Her personality, her essence, her considerable violence. Her colorful animal tattoos, the gruff way she spoke, the rough athleticism of her movements.

And instead of erasing a physical body, I erased her very essence from the room.

She disappeared from her chair. I whooped in excitement—and she answered with a high-pitched scream. The hallucination snapped and she reappeared, face white, eyes bulging, and chest heaving. She'd held on to her fork, but a glob of salmon was lying on the table.

"You—what—that—" She gulped repeatedly. "A little warning, asshole!"

Yeah, maybe warning her would've been good. I could simultaneously see my hallucinations and see through them, so even when I invisified myself, my body was still present to all my senses. What would it be like to lose all sense of yourself? To not be able to see your own body or hear your own voice or breathing or footsteps?

I let her finish eating, then excitedly resumed my experimentation. Fun for me, not for her. Even worse than losing sight of herself, her sense of touch was substantially subdued while she was invisified—a side effect I hadn't anticipated. And it turns out that when you can't see, hear, or feel your own limbs, you get *really* clumsy.

We spent the rest of the evening and the next day working on it—me building up my stamina for this new psychic skill, and Vera building up her tolerance toward the erased-self syndrome I was inflicting upon her. She had to get used to moving while invisible, touching without feeling, and talking while deaf to her own voice.

That evening, we did a test run at the local supermarket. I halluci-bombed the entire shopping area and put Vera into her unsettling state of nonexistence, then we walked around the store together, picking up more snack food.

She lifted a frozen entrée of ginger beef and asked in a strangely labored voice, "What do you want?"

"Dr. Pepper and All Dressed chips. Oh! And some cheese!"

"What are you, like, thirteen years old?"

"Make it fancy cheese, then."

She fulfilled my request with stunted movements, and we walked out of the store with an armful of deliciousness, completely undetected. A block away, I dropped the halluci-bomb. Vera reappeared. Heaving a sigh of relief, she passed me a Dr. Pepper.

I cracked the can open and took a swig. "Are we ready?"

She shrugged. "As ready as we'll ever be."

A glowing endorsement if I'd ever heard one.

17

HEIST DAY. Who was excited? Vera definitely was. Me ... not so much. But this was the price for a handcuff-free trip out of the country.

With the morning sun peeking through a thin layer of clouds that would thicken into gloomy overcast by midafternoon, I climbed onto Vera's motorcycle behind her and we made the trek across the bay and back into the city. Faustus's sale was scheduled for that night, and we aimed to be at his restaurant by noon.

Why not sneak in during the sale and use a few good hallucinations to hide our greedy mitts snatching up Vera's artifacts? Because there'd be way too many people, way too much chance for error, and way too much extra security for the very purpose of foiling thieves.

So, being oh so clever, we'd steal her artifacts back *before* the sale. No way could that go wrong.

I was chewing the inside of my cheek as the bike rolled to a stop at a red light on the Eastside. On the corner across the intersection was a cube-shaped brick building with an unwelcoming front door tucked into a shadowy nook. I squinted at it.

"Hey, I think I've seen that place before," I shouted over the rumble of the bike's motor. "It's a bar, right?"

Vera shook her head. "You don't wanna go there."

"Isn't that where they filmed *Deadpool*?"

"That's a guild—the Crow and Hammer."

A ping of dread struck me. Okay, not a cool film location. The Crow and Hammer was the guild that had toasted KCQ into blackened debris, then ground what remained—including my not-so-bad life—into dust under their fancy-pants combat boots. KCQ might have picked that fight, but the Crow and Hammer had sure as hell finished it.

I didn't know much about the guild, but I did know I didn't want to hang around and find out if they might recognize a KCQ escapee. With a casual glance around, I dropped a quick halluci-bomb on every vehicle in sight and turned all the traffic lights red.

Tires squealed as half a dozen shocked drivers slammed the brakes.

"Go," I called to Vera.

"The light—"

"Just do it!"

She hit the gas. With a rubbery screech, we were across the empty intersection, and I dropped the hallucination. Horns honked angrily as we accelerated away from the Crow and Hammer—and toward Faustus Trivium. It felt like an "out of the frying pan and into the fire" situation.

I briefly questioned the judiciousness of my life choices, then swatted the notion away. Now was not the time for wisdom. Now was the time for charging headfirst into the lair of a dangerous criminal!

We stashed the bike between a dumpster and a compost bin a couple blocks away from Corky's and walked the rest of the way. Before we were within eyesight of the restaurant, we paused in a sheltered nook behind a dumpster.

Step One: The Anti-Vera Halluci-Bomb.

I deployed the mass projection, effectively wiping Vera out of existence. She and her jean jacket, camo pants, and canvas backpack disappeared in the eyes of everyone except me. She sucked in a steadying breath as all her senses went wonky.

"I still don't … like this," she muttered, holding her hands out in front of her.

We resumed our approach. By the time we reached Corky's, her gait almost resembled that of a normal, functioning human being.

I sniffed the rancid air wafting out the door and asked in an undertone, "Are you sure they serve actual food here?"

She scrunched her nose. "Maybe just order coffee."

I opened the door with enough gusto for her to slip in after me.

The inside of Corky's Cuisine didn't smell any better than the outside, nor did the décor inspire confidence in its culinary competence. The tables looked like the wobbly leftovers from other dive bars, while the chairs had definitely been stolen from the defective bin behind an unguarded Walmart.

My shoe stuck to the tiled floor, and I employed considerable effort not to make an "ew" face at the mysteriously tacky brown substance I'd walked through. A rough, handwritten note stapled to the wall instructed me to seat myself, so I chose the least rickety table I could find in the loneliest corner of the restaurant.

Vera trailed behind me. "You're sure none of them can see me?"

We both looked across Corky's distinctly male patronage. Five men were crowded around a single table in the corner opposite mine, and none of them seemed to know what a razor was. They spoke to one another in an eloquent language of grunts.

"Kind of a sausage party, isn't it?" I observed.

"Yeah. A greasy one."

A man in his sixties, roughly the same size and shape of an elderly orangutan, lumbered out of the kitchen and crossed to my table. "Whattya want?"

"Just coffee for now."

"That it?"

"For now."

The aproned orangutan muttered something unkind and walked away, never once looking in Vera's direction. As he disappeared into the kitchen, she relaxed.

"It's working," I murmured, trying not to move my lips too much. "Either that or he's incapable of acknowledging anyone without a Y chromosome."

She surveyed the dude-centric room again. "Faustus does tend to run a bit of a boy's club. How far does your illusion thingy extend?"

"As long as you stay inside the restaurant, you'll be okay."

"You're sure?"

"A hundred percent."

She stood there for a moment longer, then shook her head. "I'm not getting any visions, so I guess we're good to go."

"Then run along," I urged her. "The faster you are, the sooner you can return to your visible form."

To be honest, I was less concerned with her personal comfort than my endurance. I wasn't sure how long I could keep the halluci-bomb going.

With a quick nod, she moved away from the table and navigated her way through the restaurant.

Step Two: Hide and Seek.

Our success was solely in Vera's hands now. All I had to do was sit still and maintain the projection while she stealthily searched the building for Faustus's stash of artifacts.

This part of our plan was comparatively weak when stacked up against the idea of posing as potential buyers, where the artifacts would be on display and easy to access. She'd have to comb the bowels of Corky's for clues, and being invisible, she had to be careful while moving about. She couldn't shift anything, including doors, if anyone might see it.

And the biggest potential obstacle: if her artifacts were sealed inside a magically reinforced piggy bank or otherwise inaccessible, then we were screwed. And that, of course, would lead to …

Step Three: Improvise.

Orangutan-man pushed through the door, carrying a plate of weirdly slimy chicken wings, and Vera slipped into the kitchen unnoticed. The server/cook/primate delivered the poultry limbs to the beefy men in the other corner, then returned to his greasy domain in the back.

Well, nothing for me to do now but maintain the projection and relax. The more energy I conserved, the better. I closed my eyes and focused on my breathing. In and out, slow and deep.

Several quiet minutes passed, then my respiratory concentration was interrupted by the odor of something that resembled sour coffee. I looked up to see that my order had arrived—only it wasn't the orangu-man who'd delivered it.

Standing in front of me was a fellow with long, straight, jet-black hair that clung to his skull and hung down to his elbows. His clean-shaven, birdlike face made it difficult to pinpoint his age. Thirty-five? Seventy-five? Probably somewhere in between. Everything, from his nose to his shoulders to the pattern on his blazer, was bizarrely geometric. Even his blindingly white grin was too triangular to be natural.

"I don't believe we've met," he said in a voice that registered somewhere between a whisper and a squeak. He extended his hand toward me. "My name is Faustus. Faustus Trivium."

18

IT TOOK ME A COUPLE OF SECONDS to fully absorb who and what I was looking at. Faustus Trivium. The very artifact dealer we were here to steal from. The one whose reputation was nasty enough to make Vera nervous. The guy who was hosting a "stolen magic" auction for the city's criminals tonight.

Yeah, him.

I reached out and completed the handshake. "I'm Kit."

Should I have used a fake name? Probably, but I was channeling most of my brainpower elsewhere at the moment.

Faustus's strange smile widened. This guy didn't resemble a single "thuggish criminal" stereotype. He looked more like a combination of Skrillex, Tilda Swinton, and a box of Wheat Thins.

He pulled out the chair across from me. "Mind if I sit?"

I shrugged, and he delicately set himself down on the chair, crossing one leg over the other and folding his hands in his lap.

"I own this place," he told me, still wearing that grin.

Great info, except I already knew that. Why had he stopped to talk to me? Did he suspect something? My mind raced through the possibilities, which wasn't good. A racing mind tuckers out a hell of a lot faster than the non-racing variety, and I had a halluci-bomb to maintain.

"That must keep you busy," I replied, unable to come up with anything more intelligent.

"Occasionally. But I have other interests that take up more of my time."

"Oh?"

"I'm a collector. I collect things."

I was aware of that too, but I feigned ignorance. "Like what? Antiques?"

His triangle smile got colder and the edges got harder. "Don't be cute, Kit. I know what you are."

My blood chilled, and I forced a slow breath through my nostrils. I couldn't panic. Not yet. "What do you mean?"

"You're a mythic." He reached into the collar of his turtleneck and withdrew a gaudy gold chain. Dangling off it was a diamond-encrusted compass that couldn't possibly point north. "I won this artifact in a game of poker a few years ago. It alerts me when another mythic is in its presence, and it detected you the moment you set foot in my restaurant. You must have a powerful mythic essence about you."

"Oh, thank you." I flashed a charming smile that I hoped hid my relief. I'd set off his magical metal detector and he was coming over to check me out. That was all. He was clueless otherwise. Praise Cthulhu.

"So, what are you?" he quizzed. "What class?"

Wow. Just asking me outright? Rude.

There were five classes of magic. Spiritalis, which comprised the nature-loving, fae-worshipping witches and druids. Arcana, which included sorcerers like Lienna, as well as potion-specialist alchemists and healers. Demonica, which was made up of lunatics who thought hellish monsters made great pets. Elementaria, which consisted of element-wielding mages like my wonderful ex-cellmate.

And last but not least, Psychica. We were the mythics with abilities that weren't classical magic powers but weird brain powers, like telekinesis, telepathy, divination, dream manipulation … and whatever extra-freaky thing I was.

"But we only just met," I evaded, batting my eyelashes coyly. "At least wait for our second date before asking personal questions."

His smile didn't shift in the slightest. He was like an alien trying to imitate humans, and no one was buying it. At least, I wasn't.

"I myself am Elementaria," he informed me. "A tempemage."

I couldn't remember what a tempemage was, but I didn't let on.

"Psychica," I revealed reluctantly, keeping it vague. "So is that what you collect? Artifacts?"

"Amongst other things. You must be very powerful, Kit, or very rare to give off such a strong signal to the compass … I was all the way back in my office when you came in and you still set it off. That's unusual."

"Maybe it just knew how badly I needed this coffee."

He tucked the necklace back into his turtleneck. "So, what are you? Color me curious."

I would color him creepily persistent. I grabbed my coffee mug for the first time and took a sip. Yup. It tasted as bad as it smelled. Did they mix it with cat litter or something?

"Like I said, Faustus," I replied calmly, as though my taste buds hadn't gone into a full civil revolt. "I don't put out on a first date."

"I have a fine nose for mythical abilities." He made a sweeping gesture toward the group of grimy dudes on the opposite side of the room. "All my associates possess unique or powerful abilities. I guess you could say I've collected them as well."

There were no two ways about it—that was a super weird thing to say.

"Fascinating," I said flatly.

Faustus made a noise that might've been a laugh but resembled something closer to a pigeon being flattened by a truck. "I like to befriend mythics of all types. I find it keeps my social life more interesting. We could be good friends, Kit. I'm sure I could be useful in some way to a mythic like you."

My eyes narrowed. Hmm. Was he laboring under the assumption that I was here because I wanted something from him? That could work in my favor.

Saving my own ass was my top priority, but I hadn't forgotten about Quentin and his ambitions. The whole point of Blue Smoke was to steal an artifact, and if my former pal planned to complete that theft, I'd like to know what nasty magic I would thusly need to avoid.

And on the off chance I did find out some juicy details, maybe I *would* drop an anonymous email to one lshen@magipol.net—or whatever Lienna's email was. She could do a quick turnaround on her career after my embarrassing escape, and Quentin would get what was coming to him for screwing with Maggie's emotions. With one well-aimed stone, I'd take care of two birds that had been pecking at my conscience for days.

Daring to shift more of my brainpower away from the halluci-bomb, I focused on Faustus. "Let's circle back to artifacts. You don't merely collect them. You're a dealer."

The corners of his smile drove deeper into his cheeks. "Are you in need of an artifact, Kit? Or do you have something to sell?"

"That depends. Any dive bar owner can call himself a dealer and peddle dime-a-dozen rain detectors, but I'm looking for a higher caliber of vendor."

Was a rain detector even a thing? I had no idea, but it sounded legit.

"I assure you I am the premier dealer in the Eastside. You might find flashier trinkets at a Yamada auction, but my wares are far more unique. Exceptional. Rare, even."

A premier dealer, eh? I flicked a glance around the disgusting dining room. Somehow, I doubted that.

"I have some … *information* that would be of interest to you." I arched my eyebrows. "But I've gotta be honest here, Faustus. I suspect it's above your pay grade."

His triangular mouth reversed direction. "I doubt that, Kit. What sort of information?"

"Artifact related, obviously." I flashed a toothy grin. "I'm assuming you're familiar with Cerberus?"

His eyes widened. "You know about … I see. Impressive, Kit."

"I'm often underestimated," I replied flippantly, even though I had no idea what he meant. Lots of people knew about the security guild, so that couldn't be what had impressed him.

"Certainly, certainly. I haven't been able to uncover much—though not for a lack of connections on my part. According to the rumors, not even Cerberus has a lead on the thief."

A chill washed over me, and I hastily checked myself. I couldn't lose focus on the halluci-bomb.

Faustus's unblinking stare clung eerily to my face. "I've been watching the market for five weeks now, but the artifact has yet to appear. And with the scarcity of intelligence on the heist, I admit I have doubts that you know something of significant value about it."

"Maybe the artifact isn't on the market because the thieves are sitting on their prize," I bluffed, keeping it vague. "It isn't something you'd casually offer up for auction, after all."

"But what else would they do with it? Not use it, surely."

"You never know." I canted my head. "Do you think it's as powerful as they say?"

"Likely even more so," Faustus sniffed. "We can't know the true extent of its amplification properties, but considering the security Cerberus had applied to it, in the right hands, its power would be quite magnificent."

Amplification properties? I did not like the sound of that.

Sitting forward, I looked into his creeptastic eyes and took a shot in the dark. "I heard it's ideal for amplifying psychic powers."

"As have I." A spark lit those eyes. "Would you like to amplify your powers tenfold, Kit? Or, as Cerberus claims, twentyfold?"

The chill in my blood had reached subzero.

"No," I muttered distractedly, fighting to drag my focus off my burgeoning dread and back to the halluci-bomb. "But I know someone who would."

"A psychic?"

"The worst kind."

"Hmm."

As Faustus's geometric smile bloomed anew, I decided it was well past time to make like an amoeba and split. Where was Vera? The fuel in my psychic tank was dwindling—not helped by that healthy dose of "oh shit" fear.

"Before we proceed further, Kit, shall we discuss your abilities?" he asked with a sharp edge—one that warned me it was my turn to be forthcoming. "I'm afraid I can't broker a deal until I know."

So as to ensure I wasn't psychically gifted at deception—which I was, though not in the way he was worried about.

"My abilities," I hedged, delaying for every possible second as my gaze darted to the kitchen door.

Faustus waited several patient moments, his tolerance fading along with his pleasant expression.

I lifted my mug to my mouth and pretended to take a long sip. "They don't have a name."

And that's all it took to revive The Smile. "Fascinating! If you are the first in a new order, why, that would be an exciting discovery."

"Yeah." I could feel my grasp on the invisi-bomb slipping as worry dug its persistent tendrils in my thoughts. "Exciting."

"So? Describe your powers, Kit. I'm something of an expert in classifications."

Across the dining room, the kitchen door swung open. The orangutan lumbered out—and Vera slipped through on his heels, her backpack bulging with items she hadn't carried in with her.

Yes! Now all we had to do was make our escape.

I snapped my attention back to Faustus. "It's difficult to describe."

Vera wound between tables, her movement slow and cautious. She couldn't see herself, making navigation difficult. I knew she couldn't go any faster, but I needed her to hurry. My brain was getting foggy, like I'd just woken up from a deep sleep—a warning sign that I was maxing out my mental stamina.

"I could demonstrate," I drawled slowly, suppressing a flinch when Vera's backpack grazed a chair, "but that tends to freak people out."

Faustus was nearly drooling on the tabletop. Geez. This was inching into verbal foreplay, and I wanted to hang up the figurative phone.

"You can go ahead and demonstrate," he breathed. "I assure you my nerves are more than sufficient for any display of power."

"Yours might be, but what about your collector's editions over there?"

As Faustus glanced at the manly posse in the corner, Vera passed by, waving at me as she headed for the door. She couldn't open it on her own. I needed to end my conversation with Faustus ASAP.

Before my foggy mind could come up with a conversation ender, he turned back to face me. A sharp-edged frown had replaced his smile, and his hand drifted to his chest. He pressed his palm against his sweater—where his mythic-detecting compass was hidden.

Oh. Oh *shit*.

Faustus's birdlike eyes darted around the room, moving back and forth across Vera. She'd frozen a dozen paces from the door, and her expression blanked as a vision of the future hit her.

"How odd," Faustus murmured, tugging on the chain around his neck. The diamond-encrusted artifact appeared from beneath his shirt. He studied it, probably wondering why he could detect a new presence. Maybe he was realizing that the reason he'd sensed my arrival so strongly wasn't because I was a super-mythic, but because I hadn't entered alone.

Vera's eyelids fluttered and emotion returned to her face—a mouth-popping expression of horror. And I knew the future was about to get ugly.

Which gave me about two minutes to change it.

"A mythic presence," Faustus mused. "Extremely close, but I don't see another mythic." His stare fixed on me. "I do not suppose you have any idea as to why that would be, do you, Kit?"

"No idea at all."

Vera stared at me, half a dozen tables between us. Her face was ashen and I knew what she was about to do. After all, it's what I'd do in her shoes.

She bolted for the door.

I gathered my fraying concentration, preparing to disguise the opening of the door—not because I wanted to save her while she ditched me, but because her being out of the way would increase my chances of escaping alive.

But when I tried to add a new projection on top of the invisibility halluci-bomb, my exhausted brain and waning power imploded inside my skull.

I sagged into my chair, the room spinning and the floor rocking like I was back on Vera's boat.

The table jerked as Faustus shot to his feet. A shout rang out, followed by a raucous clatter of chairs and stomping feet, then a crash.

My vision steadied as Vera tripped over a chair that had flown into her path. As she hit the floor, she slid backward on her stomach, dragged by an invisible force.

The goon squad was on their feet, and a six-and-a-half-foot beast the approximate weight of a buffalo was making a Darth Vader claw as he telekinetically dragged Vera away from the door. Blythe was the scariest telekinetic I'd ever met, but at three times her mass, this guy could give her a run for her money.

A face appeared in my vision. Faustus leaned over me, his triangular smile back—but completely different from before. Menace oozed from his every geometrical line.

"Interesting, Kit. I see you brought a friend." His gaze turned to Vera. "I'll deal with her before we return to our discussion of your most fascinating powers."

"VERA, DARLING," Faustus crooned. "I should have expected you. Although maybe it is you who should have expected me."

A little seer humor. Cute.

Vera stood as the goon gang circled her. I, unfortunately, wouldn't be standing to join them. The room was spinning slowly, and it took effort to keep my eyes from rolling back in my head.

I might have pushed my abilities too far.

Faustus, realizing I wasn't a threat right now, kept half an eye on my limply sprawled self as he regarded Vera and her full backpack. "Is it safe to assume you have stolen from me?"

"This shit's mine," she snapped.

"I am afraid we disagree on that."

"You can't be pissed that I took back what's mine."

His smile sharpened. "I can be, I am, and I'm sure you are aware of what happens to those unfortunate enough to land on my ugly side."

From where I sat, every side was an ugly side with this dude.

"Chucky," he said to the orangutan-like cook, "would you like to do the honors?"

The man stepped forward, looked her up and down, then gave his boss an inquisitive look. "Right now?"

"Afraid, Chucky? She's just a seer. While it is a useful ability, she has no real power."

At this particular moment, neither did I. I'd used up my psychic juice and I needed a couple minutes to recover enough to save my ass, especially if I had to target this entire collective of slime-ball mythics.

The orangutan turned his palms upward and fire ignited over his hands. Did Faustus have his enemies burned alive like Salem witches?

Vera's eyes widened, her darting gaze searching for an escape—but there was none. The pyromage raised his arms, flames streaking toward the ceiling. Furnace-like heat washed over me even from my table in the corner.

I shoved upright in my seat. "What about a trade, Faustus? My information is worth more than our lives—and Vera's goodies."

Faustus gestured at Chucky to wait, then rotated to face me. "I rather doubt that."

"The stolen Cerberus artifact. I know where it is."

He went still. "Impossible."

"Implausible," I corrected. "But I do know, and I'll tell you as soon as Vera and I are safely out of here."

The three-point smile returned. "I'm no fool, Kit. You will tell me before you or Vera set foot outside this establishment."

I pushed to my feet. The room didn't whirl like a theme park ride, and I was calling that a win. "Then we'll tell you from the door. How's that for a compromise?"

He considered it. "Agreed."

The goon squad uncircled Vera, and her wide, frightened stare bored into mine as we retreated to the door. She grasped the handle, ready to pull the door open for our escape. With my back to the exit, I faced Faustus where he stood between his telekinetic beast and pyromage ape.

"Where is the artifact, Kit?"

I swallowed. "A secret group of psychics led by KCQ's guild master stole it. It's locked in a vault in one of their offices."

"KCQ?" A greedy, manic light sparked in his eyes. "Their GM is dead."

"Yep. Almost everyone who knows about the vault and the artifact has kicked the bucket." I arched my eyebrows. "So it's finders keepers at this point."

Faustus's shiver-inducing smile bloomed over his face, and Vera yanked the door open so we could make our getaway.

Or she tried. The door didn't budge.

She wrenched on the handle. It wasn't locked. Why wasn't it opening? I grabbed the handle above her hands and pulled with all my strength. It wobbled but didn't open.

Faustus laughed.

I whipped back around—and noticed that the telekinetic beast had one hand extended. He was holding the door shut with his powers, and he was so strong that Vera and me combined couldn't overcome his mental pressure.

"I would have loved to collect you, Kit," Faustus murmured. "But it was not meant to be. Kill them."

Flames returned to the pyromage's palms, and the other men raised their hands, produced artifacts, or withdrew weapons from under their clothes.

Vera whipped something the size of a coaster out of her backpack. "*Ventos!*"

Wind burst from the artifact. The howling gust knocked the entire boys' club back on their heels and singed the eyebrows off the poor bastard standing immediately behind the pyromage.

She launched at the startled men. Her front kick slammed into the pyromage's chest, sending him sprawling into the two nearest lowlifes. Whirling, she smashed her knuckles into another man's nose. As he staggered back, a gap opened in the wall of mythics—a path to the kitchen and the unguarded back door.

Good. She had her escape route. I was using the front door—which was right behind me.

I grabbed the handle and the door swung open. A rainy breeze tasting of freedom swept over me, and I leaped across the threshold.

An invisible force clamped around my torso and hauled me backward. I flew through the air and smacked into the chest of the super-sized telekinetic. His Lou Ferrigno arms banded around me, crushing the air from my lungs. My whole skeleton creaked from the pressure.

Eyes bulging, I locked onto his mind and dropped a hallucination into his brain—the vision of flames bursting to life all over my body.

He bellowed and flung me away from him. I crashed into another guy and bounced off, unsteady on my feet. A glimpse of movement—Vera sprinting for the kitchen door.

I launched through the gap she had created, dropping my shoulder into the ribcage of a random grease-monger who got in my way. Footsteps thundered after me, and a fireball whizzed past my head.

Bursting into the kitchen, I grabbed the first thing I saw—a cast-iron skillet coated in grease, sitting beside a sink full of brown water. As the door whipped open again, I swung my weapon. It caught my pursuer—another rando—in the shoulder. He fell into the counter, blocking the doorway for the horde of goons coming in right behind him.

I sprinted deeper into the kitchen. A long counter with a grill built into it split the room in half, and my salvation—the exit—was on the far side.

"Kit!" Vera popped up from behind the counter's butt end, waving at me. "Here!"

I dove behind it, still clutching my culinary weapon. Another fireball flew past the spot where I'd been and exploded against a stockpot. The goon squad was rushing into the kitchen, and we had two seconds before they reached us.

"Can you make us invisible?" she asked desperately.

Maybe—but not for long. Sucking in a breath, I focused on Vera and myself and sent out the invisi-bomb just as the fire-wreathed orangutan rounded the counter. He peered down at the spot where we were crouched with dimwitted confusion.

"Go!" I hissed at Vera, desperately holding the projection with the fumes in my psychic gas tank.

She jumped up, and I followed, my desperation increasing as I realized my vision was going foggy—a side-effect of psychic overexertion I'd never experienced before. We sprinted for the exit.

"There!" someone shouted.

What? But my halluci-bomb was still active, wasn't it?

As I shot a panicked look over my shoulder. Vera did the same. She gasped—and I realized three things at once.

First, I hadn't included the skillet I was carrying in my halluci-bomb, meaning everyone could see it fleeing across the room all on its own.

Two, my vision wasn't going foggy. The haze was caused by the room filling with storm clouds, a bizarre sight that triggered my memory of what a "tempemage" was—a weather mage.

And three, the air was crackling in an alarming way—and I was holding a metal conductor.

"The frying pan!" Vera shrieked, but her warning came too late.

A bolt of electricity struck the pan with a loud crack. Excruciating energy surged down my arm and through my body. My muscles contracted and my jaw clenched involuntarily. After a split second, which felt like a goddamn eternity, my limbs went limp and I sagged backward, the pan clattering against the tiled floor. Vera caught me before I could fall and yanked me upright.

On the other side of the counter, Faustus smiled that creepy, ominous smile, utterly pleased with his indoor thunderstorm. "There you are."

I guess getting zapped had killed my hallucination.

His whole goon force lined the counter, and the pyromage stood only a few feet away, sparks jumping from his clenched fists. The super-telekinetic towered over Faustus, leering eagerly as he waited for the command to drag me and Vera away from the door.

I braced my feet. My brain felt like it had been slapped by a pissed-off gorilla—or maybe like it had been struck by lightning—but I gathered my shredded focus. Fatigue like I'd never felt before dragged at my mind. I'd never stretched my psychic stamina this far before.

And I was about to discover how much further I could go.

I summoned a vision of what I wanted, stretched my powers to engulf every mind except Vera's, and opened a portal to hell.

The refrigerator door morphed into a black tear in the fabric of reality, and from within that darkness, a demon crawled into view. Not a real demon—I had no idea what an actual resident of hell looked like—but my own nightmare-inducing version, inspired by every horror movie and medieval painting I'd ever laid eyes on.

It had eyes that were deep pits made of mucus and octopus tentacles.

Its skin was an oozing, scabby, bloody mess that creaked as it slunk along the floor on six misshapen limbs.

Its saliva was molten lava that leaked between its yellow, dagger-like teeth.

Its overall shape resembled an uncomfortably muscular scorpion with a humanoid body and a six-foot tail dripping venom.

The demon dropped to the sticky kitchen floor with a crunch—and the petrified goons inched backward, their faces pale and jaws slack. They couldn't take their eyes off the monster. Not one of them dared to spare a fraction of their attention to check on the thieves they'd been about to enthusiastically murder.

The only problem—it was taking so much of my shredded, exhausted concentration to hold the Creature Feature projection that I couldn't spare any thought for escaping.

Vera couldn't see the monster, but she must've realized I was doing something. She grabbed my arm and guided me backward. I stumbled blindly, gaze locked on the creature, holding it even as my vision of the rest of the room wavered and doubled.

The monster drew itself up, spreading its limbs. Its chest expanded as it drew in a deep breath. Faustus and the goons went rigid with panic.

Door hinges creaked. The damp breeze hit my back as Vera drew me across the threshold.

Just before my line of sight cut off, I narrowed my eyes, panting with effort. The monster, poised to attack, loosed an ear-splitting roar and belched a spray of magma across the entire kitchen. Every mythic, Faustus included, dove for the floor, arms shielding their heads.

Then Vera and I were out the door. Holding my elbow in a death grip, she bolted down the alley, and I ran after her, my head spinning, stomach lurching, and limbs shaking from the mental and physical drain.

But hey, my demon-monster had been seriously freakin' scary, right?

I WAS AWARE that I was dreaming.

Or at least, I knew my surroundings couldn't possibly be real. But they felt real—and I desperately wanted them to be real.

I was back in the house I'd lived in between the ages of fourteen and sixteen. No, not house. *Home.* This place was my home, more than any foster home, group home, or apartment I'd ever lived in.

It was a slender townhouse, two stories with a basement, and squished amongst a row of identical residences. I was in the living room, a space so small I could almost touch both walls if I stretched my arms out wide. Despite its size, it still managed to fit an old, soft couch with a tacky brown and orange floral pattern.

It creaked happily as I sank into it. A warm cup of chai tea sat on the coffee table. On the table's other side was a pastel pink recliner.

And in it was Gillian.

Gillian had the most beautiful soul of any person I've ever met. She was seventy-six years old when I came to live with her. After her husband's death a decade earlier, she'd started taking in foster children. Only one at a time and only teenagers.

Nobody wants teenagers. Nobody wants to take in a kid who's already been so thoroughly screwed up that they can't find a permanent home.

Nobody except Gillian.

After I'd run away from Dwayne, a.k.a. Baron von Foster-Douche, for the fourth time, he and his wife refused to take me back. I didn't complain, though the uncertainty of moving to a new home had filled me with anxiety.

But the moment I stepped foot into Gillian's house and she greeted me with her rosy smile, I knew I was in a good place.

Some people just ooze warmth and acceptance; Gillian was exactly that kind of person. She was a churchgoing lady, and every Sunday morning she would invite me to attend a service with her, and every Sunday morning I would politely decline, which never bothered her in the least.

"The invitation is always open," she'd tell me lightly.

On the coffee table, she kept a large, leather-bound Bible—the very same one I'd rescued from my apartment, let Lienna take, and would never see again. Sometimes, Gillian would read from it, but most of the time, it had simply waited there, looking pretty.

It was on the table now, beside my cup of tea and within arm's reach of Gillian, who was sipping her own hot drink.

"I'd rather cook my own food anyway," she said. "Hospital food is the worst."

We'd talked about that more than once.

Not long after my sixteenth birthday, Gillian developed a bad cough. Just a virus, we thought at first. But it lingered, then got worse, and eventually, the doctors confirmed it was terminal lung cancer. Just like that. One minute she had a cold, the next she was only a month away from the graveyard.

I was devastated, but Gillian refused to feel sorry for herself. She was more concerned about what would happen to me than to her.

She knew the system and she knew me. She understood that the foster system had trouble placing older teenagers, and that meant I'd likely wind up in another group home or something crappy like that. She also knew my predilection for running away.

The Gillian of my dream set her tea down on the coffee table and gave me that gentle smile I remembered so well.

"If I go to a hospital and die there," she murmured, unafraid of the word "die," even though I could never bring myself to say it, "they'll take you away right then."

"But if you go to the hospital, they can help," I replied, unable to say anything but the words I'd uttered the day we'd had this conversation. "Maybe they can save you."

"Oh heavens, I don't think anyone except the Lord can save me at this point, Kit."

"But they can help. For a little while, at least."

"Sure, they could. I could be hooked up to machines with tubes down my throat and needles in my arm. And I could live like that for a little longer." She picked up her tea again. "Or I could stay in the comfort of my own home with you and enjoy what time I have left."

A deep ache grew in my stomach—the same pain I'd felt during the original conversation. That sickening feeling of inevitable loss. The helplessness, the fear, the overwhelming sadness. But it was layered in with something new. A regret that stuck through me like a long, thin pin. A yearning to hold on to the past.

"You're a beautiful boy," she said softly. "I've never told you this before, but it's your compassion that makes you beautiful. Do you know that?"

"What do you mean?"

"You hurt when you see others hurt. You want to help them so badly it drives you crazy. That's a beautiful quality. I won't be around much longer to remind you of that, so I want you to promise me that you won't forget it." She took another sip of her tea, as if that would punctuate her statement. "Do you understand, Kit? Promise me you won't forget."

I picked up my tea and held it close to my face to hide the way my lips trembled. "I won't. I won't forget."

Those words twisted the needle of remorse.

"Life will be hard on you," she continued. "We both know that. You're going to run away again. You're almost a grown man, so I think you should." Her eyes, framed by softly wrinkled skin, met mine. "Run, Kit. Find a place in this world and claim it. You have incredible gifts, and you should use them to make your way."

I'd never fully divulged my abilities to Gillian, partly because I couldn't shake the fear that it would scare her away and partly because I hadn't understood them well enough to explain what I could do. But she'd known me better than anyone and she'd accepted it all, weird quirks and possible supernatural abilities included.

She sipped her tea. "But no matter what happens, you won't lose your compassion, will you?"

"No," I promised solemnly, "I won't."

"That makes me so happy to hear. You will always be such a beautiful boy." She perked up at the thought. "Oh, a beautiful *man* someday too!"

She laughed delightedly, and all I could think was that she hadn't lived to see me grow into a man.

I wanted her to keep talking. Hearing her voice, that light, youthful cadence sprinkled with the odd crack that betrayed her age, was inexplicably warming even as it drove spikes of anguish into my chest.

Seeing her hurt. Dreaming this memory hurt so much because I knew she was gone. Three weeks after this conversation, I said my last goodbye to her.

In her final moments, when her lungs were failing and she struggled for every gasp, I sat beside her bed, gripped her hands, and gave her a hallucination to comfort her.

A sun-bathed beach in Hawaii. Aquamarine water rushing across white sand with that soft sound that only waves meeting a gentle shore could make. I made the sun hot, the sand cool, and the sky the clearest crystal blue I could imagine. A handsome cabana boy stood nearby with a palm frond, offering us shade and providing a view that Gillian unabashedly admired.

She'd always wanted to go to Hawaii but could never afford it because she'd spent all her time and money taking care of dumb runaways like me. So, I took her there.

It was the only time in my life I'd created a hallucination like that. Immersive and complete. I've tried to replicate it since but have always failed.

We sat there together, basking in the hallucination and enjoying the weather and the beauty, until her mind faded …

and no matter how far I stretched my psychic senses, I couldn't find her again.

I CAME TO WITH A VIOLENT START.

Bittersweet grief and guilt churned in my gut, left over from the dream—but those emotions were cut short by the realization that I was falling.

A fraction of a second later, I hit the ground, landing on my shoulder and hip. I groaned from the impact, but my mouth was so dry that only a scratchy whisper came out. The familiar interior of Vera's boat greeted my eyes, the bed beside me with blankets twisted across it.

Two important details struck me: first, the boat was bouncing up and down and side to side, which meant we were no longer tied up at the dock in Deep Cove; and second, I was wearing nothing but my underwear.

Thankfully, my clothes were hanging off a nearby chair. The same clothes I'd been wearing for several intense days. I needed a washing machine.

I picked up my shirt and gave it a cautious sniff. A faint hint of citrus surprised me. I got dressed, chugged a bottle of water I'd found in the mini-fridge, and made my way up to the deck. The sun was low in the sky, but between the misty weather and landmark-free open water surrounding us, I had no idea if it was just past dawn or almost dusk.

Vera was in the captain's chair, hand on the wheel as she watched me take a few uneasy steps toward her on the rocking deck. "Hey there. How're you feeling?"

"Groggy. How long was I out?"

"About five hours. It's just after six p.m." She eyed me with concern. "I tried to wake you up a few times, but you weren't having it. Do you normally sleep like that after using your abilities?"

No, but I'd never pushed myself that far before. I'd only just learned how to make another person invisible, and I'd never needed to hold a halluci-bomb for so long either. Also, my life didn't usually depend on my projections.

Thanks to those special circumstances, I'd found out my limits weren't where I'd thought they were—and I'd also discovered that shooting past my psychic ceiling came with consequences. Such as sleeping like the living dead and experiencing painfully vivid memory-dreams.

Instead of admitting all that, I took a few more awkward steps and plunked myself in the seat next to Vera. "Did you wash my clothes?"

"They were getting ripe. I didn't do your underwear, though. I don't know you well enough for that."

"That's fair. You got all your artifacts?"

"Yep."

That's all she said, and I let the silence take hold. No point in bringing up how she'd tried to ditch me, then I'd tried to ditch her, then we'd somehow both escaped certain death despite the odds being stacked against us in the biggest way.

I looked out at the grayish-blue waves. We were speeding through choppy water, but the mist obscured everything more than fifty yards out. If I squinted, I could make out what might be the faint silhouette of land.

"Where are we going?" I asked after a minute.

"I'm delivering you to a cargo ship a few miles off Bowen Island. They'll take you across the Pacific and connect you with my guy in the Philippines, who'll set you up with a new identity."

My gut flip-flopped unpleasantly. "The Philippines?"

"Yeah, but you don't have to live there. My guy can advise you on your options. Australia is trickier, but you could make it happen."

I nodded slowly. Australia didn't sound so bad. I could totally learn an Aussie accent and blend in like a local in no time.

"Vera …" I hesitated. "Can I borrow your phone?"

"Why?"

"Need to Google something."

She fished her cell from her pocket and handed it to me. I typed a quick search query, then waited an agonizing thirty seconds for the results to load.

Moonphases.org gave me the answer I was looking for: the next "waning third crescent moon," the only night each month that Rigel's uncrackable vault could be opened, would happen … tonight.

Tonight, Quentin would have Maggie open the secret vault she'd created for Rigel, in which was stored the terrifying artifact Blue Smoke had stolen from Cerberus five weeks ago. I'd thought Quentin had planned to complete the theft, but he didn't need to. Blue Smoke had already done it.

All Quentin had to do was claim the prize for himself.

I looked up. Through the fog, the shadow of an enormous cargo ship took shape. The ship that would take me away from all of this insanity, out of the grip of the MPD, and thousands of miles from my old life.

This was it. Safety. No more jail cells, sentencing hearings, or possible dates with an executioner. I had successfully survived the collapse of KCQ, escaped the MPD, and negotiated transport with a smuggler. I'd swum naked through the ocean and stolen from an illegal artifact dealer to get here.

My freedom was on the horizon, but …

I couldn't believe that sentence contained a "but." Yet there it was. A big one.

My freedom was on the horizon, but it came at a price I hadn't expected. No, not risking my life to steal Vera's artifacts. These costs weren't ones *I* had to pay.

Lienna Shen, who against her better judgment had shown me kindness, respect, and the beginnings of trust when they were entirely scarce in my life, would pay for my freedom with her career. I'd undermined her position as an agent, betrayed her faith in me, and left her at the mercy of her vengeful, authoritarian captain.

Maggie Cook, who'd befriended me when I was new to the city and completely alone, who'd invited me over for Christmas, and who'd given me gentle guidance in this dangerous new world of mythics, would pay for my freedom with her life. She'd fallen into Quentin's psychopathic hands, and I'd done nothing to help her. After tonight, he wouldn't need her anymore. With the prize he was about to claim, he wouldn't leave any loose ends alive.

And finally, an unknown number of nameless, faceless people would pay for my freedom once Quentin, the most powerful empath anyone had ever seen, held an artifact that could amplify his powers twentyfold. He'd be unstoppable.

I was the only one who knew his plan.

My eyes slid closed. The urge to run, to flee, to get on that cargo ship and never look back pounded through me. Gillian had told me I would run away. She'd accepted it. She'd been okay with it.

But no matter what happens, you won't lose your compassion, will you?

Hard years had followed her death, each one full of people who'd rejected me, deceived me, used me, or just flat out didn't give a damn about me. And at some point between then and now, I'd broken my promise. I'd stopped caring about anyone but myself.

I opened my eyes. The shadow of the cargo ship had grown clearer.

"I can't," I groaned miserably.

Vera looked over. "Can't what?"

"I can't do this. I need to go back."

Her jaw dropped. "You're kidding, right?"

I took one last look at the ship—at my escape—and shook my head. "I wish I was."

"YOU'RE CRAZY," Vera informed me.

I had to agree.

"You sure you want to do this?"

Not at all.

"We can return to my boat."

Teeth clenched, I swung off her motorcycle. "I've got to do this. I explained why."

She pushed her helmet visor up. "You don't owe anyone anything, Kit."

From where I was standing, it felt like I owed a lot of people quite a bit. Even if I could ignore screwing over Lienna, whom I'd only known for a few days, and even if I could ignore my friendship with Maggie, who was a grown woman and technically responsible for herself, I couldn't fail Gillian. She'd sacrificed her final few years to give me a chance to become someone better than a guy who'd run away from *this*.

Vera scanned my face. "Well, if you make it through the next day without landing behind bars again, have Jenkins contact me. I still owe you a one-way ticket off this continent."

I nodded, even though I knew the chances of that were well below zero.

She stared into the distance, then revved the motorcycle's engine. "By the way, if you waltz your noble ass in there right now, your little agent friend is going to walk out of the elevator, spot you, and put you down with a spell in two seconds flat. Just FYI."

I stared at her. "That's my future? You saw it?"

"Just now." She arched her eyebrows, then slid her visor down. "Good luck."

With another snarl, the bike squealed away from the curb. Vera zoomed into the evening traffic, leaving me standing on the sidewalk beside the MPD precinct's shared parking garage.

Well, shit. I sure could've used more of that seer forewarning, but at least I knew what to expect in the next five minutes.

I released a halluci-bomb on every mind in my vicinity, making myself invisible to all eyes, then slunk down the ramp, past the ticket machine, and into the dim garage interior. Passing a silver BMW and a truly gorgeous Maserati—not the MPD vehicles, obviously—I ducked behind a thick pillar.

Just past the concrete support was the battle-ready fleet of the world's most secret and powerful organization: six MPD smart cars. And just past those was the door to the elevators where, according to Vera's vision, Lienna was about to appear.

Last I'd checked, it was just after eight o'clock. Counting travel time, it was probably around eight thirty. A late end to the day for a rookie agent, but Lienna was probably trying to make up lost ground after my escape.

I'd barely planned my next move before the elevator doors opened and Lienna walked out. Her satchel was hooked over her shoulder, beads clinking in her raven ponytail and an assortment of jewelry hanging around her neck—including her anti-magic cat's eye pendant, which I'd abandoned on the café table before escaping. She had to activate it for it to block my magic, and she had no reason to do that while walking out to her car.

She didn't look threatening, one arm cradling a Blythe-like stack of folders while she felt around her coat pockets for car keys. Her shoulders had an exhausted, almost defeated hunch that I'd never seen before.

Ignoring a squirm of guilt, I focused on her mind. As she walked up to the driver's door of her car, I brought a vision to life.

The elevator door chimed again. Blythe strode out, wavy blond hair blowing back from her face and her mouth pressed thin. She strode toward the line of cars.

"Agent Shen!" she barked.

Lienna recoiled as her superior bore down on her. "Captain Blythe? I thought you'd left for the day."

Oh, oops. I'd assumed Blythe was a cyborg who didn't eat, sleep, or go home at night.

"Is something wrong?" she added.

"Obviously," Blythe growled, continuing toward the young agent. "We have a problem to discuss."

"What's that?"

Fake-Blythe said nothing. She didn't have anything to discuss with Lienna, but I did—and while my Cap-tastic projection had been delaying Lienna from getting in her car, I'd snuck up behind her, still invisible.

Letting Fake-Blythe disappear, I pulled Lienna's satchel off her shoulder and slung it away from us.

She whipped around, folders spilling to the concrete floor as her hands rose defensively. I caught her wrists and pushed her back into the car. With a twist of her arm, she freed one hand—and drove her fist into my gut.

Oof. Yeah, I deserved that.

As gently as possible, I body-checked her into the car. Catching her free arm again, I pinned her with my larger size and weight. She squirmed violently, trying to break my hold, but I had a good grip.

She stomped on my foot and when I flinched, she almost landed a headbutt.

"Lienna!" I gasped. "Just hold still for a second!"

"Let me go!" she yelled furiously. "You lying, cheating son of a—"

I mashed her harder into the car before she pushed me off balance.

"Was escaping not good enough for you?" she snarled, viciously kicking my ankles. "You came back for some revenge too?"

"No! I came back because I need your help."

"*My help?* What makes you think I'd *ever*—"

"Because if we don't stop Quentin, he's going to kill Maggie and escape with an artifact that can amplify his abilities by twenty."

She stopped struggling, and I panted from the effort of holding her—and from the throbbing bruises she'd inflicted. I should've gotten my explanation out faster.

Her chest heaved, and we both paused to catch our breath, our faces inches apart as I pinned her to the car door with my body. Fury burned in every line of her face, giving her glaring brown eyes a breathtaking intensity that was both surprisingly attractive and freakin' intimidating.

"Explain," she said flatly.

I exhaled in a rush. "Blue Smoke was a plan Rigel hatched to steal something from the security guild Cerberus. It's an artifact that can amplify psychic magic."

"An artifact?" she muttered.

"Before the heist, Rigel hired Maggie to create a hidden vault in his office where he could store the stolen artifact. That was her role in Blue Smoke."

"Wait. Does that mean the artifact is in this vault? Right now?"

"I'm ninety-nine percent sure. Maggie is the only person still alive who knows how to get into the vault, and Quentin got to her before we did. When I escaped with her"—Lienna's glare quadrupled in meanness, and I suppressed a wince—"she ran straight to Quentin. He's convinced her that they're madly in love."

Lienna's jaw clenched and unclenched as she absorbed all that. "So you found this out when you talked to Maggie, then sat on the information for three days? Why are you coming to me now?"

"I only found out about the stolen artifact early this afternoon and realized what it meant. I came to you as soon as I could. I was sort of unconscious until a couple hours ago."

"Unconscious? What happened?"

"Not important." I loosened my grip on her wrists. "Lienna, I know I was a selfish ass, but I couldn't face possible execution. I'm back now because—"

"Execution?" she interrupted disbelievingly. "You thought you might be *executed*? For a few counts of fraud?"

"*Sixty-one* charges, Lienna. Of which a large portion aren't even legit, according to you. They levied those charges to scare me. I'm betting they put me in a cell with a serial killer to scare me even more. I don't know who has it out for me or why, but if they've already filed excessive charges against me, who's to say they won't give me an excessive sentence?"

She opened her mouth but didn't seem to know what to say.

"How could I risk it?" I asked quietly. "I had no one to defend me. I was at their mercy."

She caught her lower lip in her teeth.

"I came back because Quentin is going to make Maggie open that vault, and he's going to take that artifact, and he's going to use it. And when he does, it'll make the riot he caused in the precinct look like a toddler brawl in a daycare."

She drew in a deep breath, and I pretended not to notice her chest pressing into mine.

"Okay. Okay, yes, we need to stop Quentin. Do you know where to find him?"

"The vault is in Rigel's secret Blue Smoke office, and Quentin should be there by 9:15."

Her eyes popped with alarm. "You mean *tonight*? Why 9:15?"

"The sun sets at 9:15, and once the night of the third crescent moon begins, he can open the vault."

"I see." She twisted her wrists. "Let me go, Kit."

I released her arms and stepped back, oddly cold now that I wasn't pressed against her warmth. Her hand dipped into her back pocket and she pulled out her phone. The screen lit up, the time stamped across it.

8:45 p.m.

We had thirty minutes to reach the vault and stop Quentin from opening it.

ANY HOPE that we'd beaten Quentin to the fire-damaged office was extinguished the moment it came into view. Lights glowed from the hollow windows and burnt gaps in the walls.

"Shit," I muttered.

Lienna nodded tersely. The short drive hadn't been a chatty one. I'd spent most of it expanding on what I'd learned and how best to deal with Quentin. She kept gripping her cat's eye necklace as though to ensure it was still there—or maybe wishing she could activate it. I'd warned her to save the spell for when she got near Quentin.

I really wished she had a spare one for me, because I wasn't looking forward to getting within Quentin's range. I knew what he could do, and it was never a fun time.

Lienna parked in a shadowed lot half a block away, and we cautiously approached the lit-up building. Male voices rumbled from the interior, and I glanced worriedly at Lienna. Had Quentin brought backup?

Not good, because we had no backup. Another of my recommendations: Quentin's super-rage miasma made him too dangerous. With a high enough dose of hateful fury, allies could turn on one another.

We scaled the fence and crept toward the door. I peeked inside, then jerked back, mouth hanging in disbelief. Lienna leaned past me to scan the interior.

"Who are all those people?" she whispered in alarm. "You said it would be just Quentin and Maggie!"

"I … uh … I may have miscalculated."

Gulping, I peered inside again.

The burnt interior was well lit by several electric lanterns set on the floor. Shadows flickered over the charred walls as an assortment of ugly, greasy, grizzly mythics moved about with purpose.

In their center was a tall, slender, angular man with straight black hair down to his elbows.

"Keep searching," he commanded in his thin voice. "It's here somewhere."

As several grunts answered him, I retreated from the doorway and rubbed my hands over my face. Shit, shit, *shit*. Faustus didn't waste any freakin' time, did he? He was supposed to be having an artifact sale tonight, not following up on my tip about the Cerberus theft!

Unless he'd canceled the auction because Vera and I had stolen most of the spells he'd been planning to hock. And now he was on the hunt for the vault.

"So, um …" I flicked a glance at Lienna. "Have you ever heard of Faustus Trivium?"

She'd pulled out her phone and was typing furiously. "No?"

"He's an artifact dealer with a gang of hairy ape-minions, who I may or may not have tipped off about the Blue Smoke vault and the artifact inside it."

She looked up in disbelief. "Why would you do that?"

"I was attempting not to die. Speaking of which, Faustus *really* wants to kill me."

Her thumbs flew across her phone screen, then she shoved the device in her pocket and pulled out her wooden Rubik's

Cube. "We need to get to that vault. It's 9:05. We only have ten minutes before Quentin can open it."

And once he had that artifact, we—and anyone else who tried to stop him—would be helpless against his magnified power. But we couldn't just charge in there. Vera and I had barely escaped Faustus and his men this afternoon. Round Two would be even worse.

Lienna twisted her cube, aligning different runes. The light leaking from the office cast harsh shadows over her terse expression. "I can't hold off that many mythics at once, and if they—"

"Oy!"

We whipped around. From the far corner of the building, a familiar mustache in a security guard uniform scurried toward us with his hand on his holster. Trevor Eggert. The old man in a young man's body who'd interrupted us the last time we'd been here.

"What do you think you're do—"

"*Shh!*" Lienna and I hissed vehemently.

His angry approach faltered. "It's you two again. Why—"

"*Quiet!*" Lienna snapped in a whisper.

"What're you doing, Eggsy?" I demanded in a low tone. "You shouldn't be here."

"I absolutely should be here," he countered, mimicking our whispers. "I'm the night guard. And badge or not, you two can't just—"

"You need to leave," Lienna ordered. "This situation is—"

"Faustus!" a voice bellowed from inside.

Eggert tried to step around me. "Who's in there?"

"Found something!" the same goon shouted eagerly.

"Found what?" Eggert muttered. "What's a faustus?"

Cursing under my breath, I elbowed him back and peeked inside again. Faustus and several of his men were clustered around the wide steel pillar that concealed the secret entrance to Rigel's underground office. They'd found the rune that unlocked the hidden door.

I whipped back to face Eggert. "Listen, Eggsy. Shit's about to get ugly. In there right now is a nasty guy with a whole bunch of other nasty guys trying to do nasty things."

"Shouldn't you stop them? And what's a faust—"

"Just stay out of the way." Unable to waste any more time on the human, I inched into the doorway. "Lienna, don't react to anything you're about to see. Things are gonna get weird."

"What do you mean?" she asked nervously.

I couldn't spare the brainpower to exclude her mind. Gathering my focus, I pictured what I wanted—then unleashed a halluci-bomb on everyone around me.

As Faustus eagerly examined the rune, the metal began to glow with nonexistent heat. I couldn't add any sensation to go with the visual, but the men recoiled anyway. The pillar glowed more and more brightly, the air rippling with heat waves that had no heat, then the whole thing melted like candle wax.

The metal slumped in a goopy, molten puddle, and Faustus stumbled backward, hands raised as though tempted to try reforming its shape.

"What happened?" he barked.

A tug on my jacket almost distracted me—Lienna was clutching the fabric as she leaned over my shoulder to peer into the room.

"Kit," she whispered faintly. "What …"

Keeping the pillar invisified—good thing I'd practiced that so much—and maintaining the vision of the molten metal, I focused on a burnt hole in the floor. Light shimmered over it, and a glowing staircase appeared, leading downward.

Faustus whirled toward the light. "There! That's it!"

The nice thing about magic: when people know it exists, they're way more prone to believing far-fetched nonsense.

As he and his men approached it, I reached back and grabbed Lienna's arm. Drawing her with me, I crept through the doorway. Eggert, thankfully, didn't try to follow us—probably too unnerved by the hallucinatory magic I was tossing around.

Faustus and his men murmured over the glowing stairway, then Creepazoid gestured imperiously. One of his cronies inched closer, peered at the imaginary staircase, then took a bold step down.

His foot passed right through the illusion and he shrieked as he fell into the unseen basement. He landed with a loud crunch.

Lienna and I darted through the shadows along the wall. As Faustus recoiled from the not-a-staircase, I made it dissolve into light, revealing a black pit in the floor. The edges crumbled inward and the hole spread into a yawning chasm of darkness.

The men scrambled backward, shouting in alarm.

"What is this?" Faustus screeched.

As Lienna and I scooted past, she reached down and flicked off a nearby lantern, deepening the shadows. I increased the speed at which the hole was crumbling, hoping the men would run for it. We reached the pillar, and Lienna blindly stretched her hands out, finding the cold metal she could no longer see.

Faustus and his men retreated, tripping and stumbling on the debris-strewn floor. Fear clung to them. They were about to break.

Then Chucky the orangutan pyromage tripped over one of his overlarge feet. He pitched backward, caught himself, and lurched forward. He staggered for balance—and stepped squarely on the dark emptiness.

And, of course, his foot landed on the non-chasm floor, because it was all a hallucination.

"What—?" Faustus gasped.

Lienna slid her hands frantically over the invisible pillar, searching for the rune. I racked my brain for a new distraction, but Faustus's head came up. He whirled around.

Our eyes met from across the room, and I braced for that whole pile of "ugly" I'd warned Eggert was coming.

"KIT MORRIS." Faustus smiled his three-point smile. "You are indeed a rare and fascinating mythic—and soon to be a dead one." He waved at his goons. "Kill him!"

A dozen mythics of varying classes, power, viciousness, and greasiness turned on Lienna and me. They unleashed their magic.

I made myself disappear. As Lienna gasped in shock, I yanked her behind the pillar, which fizzled back into view as my concentration went in a different direction—the "not dying" direction.

A maelstrom of magic and flying weapons blasted past the spot where we'd been standing. Sorcery, magery, and who knew what else hit the wall and exploded in a rainbow of sparks and debris.

I dropped the invisibility hallucination. Lienna goggled at me.

"You didn't explain your power very well last time, did you?" she growled, pressed against the pillar.

"I did explain." I stuck my head around the steel barrier keeping us from being barbequed, and with a second's concentration, made the debris-strewn floor turn into an amusement park's best funhouse room—bold, foot-high ripples of shiny black plastic. The advancing horde of mythics stumbled, staggered, and fell as they either tripped over the invisible debris or tried to step on waves that weren't there.

"I can make people see hallucinations," I added, breathless with brain-numbing focus. "Not my fault you lack imagination and assumed changing paint color was all I could do."

"Not 'hallucinations.' Warps."

"Huh?"

"Your magic—it's a rare ability called psycho warping." She gave me an eye roll that didn't seem appropriate considering Faustus's death squad was headed our way. "I looked it up after you used your magic to escape."

My jaw hung open. No way. My powers had a name?

Not flimsy hallucinations after all. I was *warping minds*, and that was a hundred times cooler. I wasn't a freak or the weird foster kid or that KCQ intern who did some kind of illusion magic. I was a psycho warper—

"It's all an illusion!" Faustus shouted. "Ignore it!"

—who'd forgotten what he was supposed to be doing.

Swearing, I peeked around the pillar. Faustus and his men had spread out on both sides of the room and were closing in on us. Nowhere to run. Nowhere to hide. And I didn't think my hallucinations—my warps—would distract them again.

I glanced at Lienna. I knew her at least as well as Vera. I could probably make her invisible—but it had taken hours for

Vera to adjust to losing half her senses. No way could I do that to Lienna in the middle of a fight.

Warning pinged through my brain, and I realized the air had gone misty. Clouds formed at the ceiling. The air sizzled.

I grabbed Lienna around the middle and vaulted away from the metal pillar.

Three bolts of lightning leaped from the clouds and struck the pillar. The current sizzled down the steel and into the floor, buzzing across my nerves as Lienna and I hit the ground.

Mythics charged in from every direction. Fire, glowing artifacts, swords, and blades—they all pointed our way, attacks about to rip us apart.

Lienna thrust her Rubik's Cube into the air. "*Ori te formo cupolam!*"

A watery blue dome expanded from the cube, encasing us, and the volley of magical assaults slammed into the barrier. It rippled wildly.

Standing behind his men, Faustus raised his hand. The clouds above Lienna's dome condensed, darkening to an angry gray. Light flickered in their depths—another round of lightning about to strike. On our left, Chucky the pyromage built an inferno on his palms. Another man raised his sword. A sorcerer pointed a wand at us.

I clamped my arms around Lienna, knowing their combined attacks would shatter the barrier—and our bodies.

A sharp wolf whistle rang through the room.

"Heyo!" With a crunch of footsteps, a woman skipped down the stairs from the building's barely standing upper level. She hopped the last few steps, landed with a thump a few feet behind Faustus, and swung a huge bastard sword up onto her shoulder like a baseball bat.

I blinked confusedly at the petite woman's pink-streaked blond hair and leather corset crisscrossed with the straps of her baldric. I'd never seen her before.

She flashed a grin. "Take a look at this bunch. We've got some ugly ones."

A second woman descended the steps behind the first. Early fifties, iron-gray hair, the sort of mouth that never smiled. In her wake came a tall Black woman with her long hair braided and tied into a high ponytail. Last but not least, a woman with vaguely Slavic features stopped several steps above the other three, her imperious stare sweeping the room.

"Agent Shen?" she called calmly.

Lienna, crouched on the floor with my arms wrapped protectively around her, a shield glowing over us, and surrounded by a horde of goons about to rain down hell, cleared her throat. "That's me."

"Tabitha Boden, second officer, Crow and Hammer. We're here to assist."

I blinked a few more times. A guild team? Here to *assist?*

The memory of Lienna typing rapidly on her phone popped into my head. *Oh.* She'd called for backup after seeing it wouldn't be two-on-two but two-on-twelve. Nice of her to share that little detail.

Though that explained *why* the team was here, it didn't explain how they'd gotten onto the upper level to make their approach right into the rogues' midst—until I spotted a flicker of movement. Peeking from behind Tabitha was a ruffled mustache.

Eggert? He'd led them to the upper level?

Sneering, Faustus waved dismissively at the heavily armed woman a step away from him. "Another foolish illusion," he barked. "Break that shield and kill them!"

His men pulled themselves together, ignoring the quartet of combat mythics only steps away. For a moment, the women looked utterly bewildered. Probably not a reaction they'd ever gotten before.

"Begin," Tabitha ordered.

The oldest woman flung half a dozen metal sticks at the men and each one burst into a tangle of red lines that ensnared their limbs. The tall woman with braids pointed her quarterstaff. Water coalesced out of nothing and a wave splashed across the floor. As it rushed over the mythics' feet, Tabitha spun a pair of billy clubs.

The wave of water froze solid, encasing half the men's feet. With a sharp grin, the petite one with the huge sword launched for the disoriented men, her blade's deadly edge shining.

And all hell broke loose.

Light flashed, magic exploded, and the air crackled with competing powers. Lienna shoved her cube at me and whipped out a handful of her stun marbles. The attacking guild team had successfully distracted over half of Faustus's men, but the rest were keen on delivering me some painful payback.

The monstrous telekinetic raised his arm and a charred desk rose into the air. With a wave, he flung it at our shield—and Lienna threw a stun marble.

"*Ori dormias!*" she yelled.

The marble hit him at the same time his desk hit our shield. The barrier shattered and I yanked Lienna clear of the falling furniture. It crashed down with a bang so loud it momentarily drowned out the cacophony filling the room. The telekinetic keeled over backward.

Out of the haze, a guy I'd whacked with a cast-iron skillet charged us, a glowing baseball bat in his hands. I lunged to meet him, ducking an instant before he could Babe Ruth my skull. My shoulder slammed into his chest, and as he staggered, I yanked the back of his shirt over his head and slammed a punch into his face through the fabric.

For a second time in one day, he went down from a blow I'd delivered. Nice.

Unfortunately, my knuckles weren't as hard as a frying pan, and the still-conscious mythic thrust his bat into the pit of my stomach. All the air disappeared from my lungs and I stumbled back, clutching my gut.

"*Ori dormias!*"

A flying marble accompanied Lienna's shout. It smacked the mythic in the chest and he went limp—but I didn't have a moment to feel relief as heat washed over my back.

Lienna and I whirled around as Chucky the pyromage bore down on us, his entire body covered in flames. Glee lit his ugly face as white-hot fireballs filled his palms. Lienna threw her last marble at him, but it missed.

The mage's left leg buckled. As he dropped to one knee, Eggert appeared behind him, his baton swinging again. The metal pole cracked against the pyromage's skull.

Lienna popped up beside me and swung our previous opponent's bat. It hit Chuck's head on the opposite side. His fire puffed out, and he collapsed.

Eggert scurried over to me, his baton still aimed at the pyromage. "Got him! Was that a demon?"

I could only half hear him over the noisy battle all around us. "Not exactly."

"Is it the faustus?"

"Nope." I looked around for the actual Faustus but couldn't see him through the haze and chaos. "Where—"

"Tabitha!" Lienna shouted so suddenly I jumped.

A woman shot out from said chaos, ice crystals sparkling on her billy clubs. "Agent Shen?"

"We need to get to that pillar." Lienna pointed at the metal structure, which was somehow across the room—I hadn't realized the fight had driven us so far away. "There's something else happening here that we need to stop."

"We can clear a path," Tabitha replied immediately. "Team!"

Somehow—were these women enhanced super-soldiers or something?—the other three mythics from the Crow and Hammer appeared around her. I looked across them as the hydromage spun her staff, the sorceress selected a new handful of artifacts, and the pocket-sized barbarian hefted her sword. Eggert watched with feverish excitement, gripping his baton in readiness.

Fantastic. My allies now consisted of an MPD agent who wanted to imprison me, a security guard who'd just learned that magic existed, and four members of the guild that had killed my boss.

Tabitha had turned to confer briefly with her team—which allowed the remaining five goons to regain their bearings. Before they could form a strategy, I casually dropped a warp on them: redecorating a tall, skinny dude into a replica of Tabitha. It wouldn't have worked under normal circumstances, but with the air hazed and their adrenaline pumping, the other four didn't notice the weirdness of the hallucination.

With furious bellows, they charged their pal.

"What on earth—" Tabitha began in a gasp.

"Ignore that," I cut in, waving a hand. "You ready?"

In answer, she lifted her hands to shoulder height. Her hydromage comrade jabbed her staff in a strange gesture, and water coalesced out of nothing—raindrops, except they floated in the air. Tabitha's face tightened with concentration, and with a flick of one hand, she froze each droplet into a pointed shard.

With another flick, the Ice Queen hurled her chilled shards across the room. Men howled as icy needles peppered their exposed skin. The four mythics launched for the five goons— and Lienna and I bolted for the pillar.

We skidded to a stop beside it, and Lienna slapped her hand to the rune. "*Ori aperio—*"

Electricity blasted down the metal. She flew backward and crashed to the floor—and I realized the haze was more cloud than dust. Dark clouds swirled across the ceiling, electricity crackling through them.

Faustus stepped around the pillar, his pointy smile firmly in place and his hands stretched out, palms facing upward. "You will pay for this, Kit. You cannot defeat Faustus Trivium!"

Whoa buddy, that's a little melodramatic.

But Faustus backed up his evil-villain rhetoric with a blast of grape-sized hail. Wind, rain, and lightning-laden clouds billowed toward me, and I shielded my face with my arms, completely helpless against his weather barrage.

Or that would have been the extremely sad result … had that really been me.

While Split Kit impersonated a feeble psychic with zero resistance to bad weather, I grabbed the bat Lienna had dropped and swung. It struck Faustus's head with a sickening thump. His eyes went soft and he keeled over.

Oh, sweet revenge, thou art best served with a baseball bat to the skull.

"Kit!"

I whirled around. Lienna stood beside the open doorway in the pillar, darkness yawning. With a frantic glance back at the four-women team pummeling the shit out of Faustus's remaining men while Eggert skulked among the fallen, ensuring they stayed down, I dove inside and slammed the door behind me.

23

DARKNESS ENCLOSED US, the raucous noise outside deadened. I squinted as my eyes adjusted to the faint light leaking up the stairwell. What time was it? It had to be after 9:15 by now.

"It's time for your cat's eye necklace," I whispered to Lienna.

She grasped the pendant. "*Ori menti defendo.*"

Drawing in a deep breath, I pushed aside the foggy tiredness clinging to my thoughts. "I'm going to make us invisible."

She nodded tersely. I wasn't close enough to sense any minds in the underground office, so I dropped my invisibility warp-bomb on everyone in my vicinity. To my relief, Lienna faded into nothing, same as me. Woo, first try! And thanks to her anti-magic necklace, she didn't have a Vera-style freak-out over her sudden lack of body.

She glanced at herself. "Did it work?"

"Yep." I started downward, and she walked beside me, nervously adjusting her satchel on her shoulder. Our quick breaths were the only sound in the hollow stairwell. "So what's the plan?"

"We'll see if Quentin is here."

A solid first step. Maybe he'd bailed when Faustus had crashed the place.

"And if he is," she added, "we'll take him down—*without* triggering that alchemy trap."

"Aw, but that was so much fun."

I could scarcely see her face in the dim light, but I didn't miss her eye roll. Damn, I loved that exasperated expression of hers. I hadn't noticed the suppressed amusement at first, but it was easy to see now.

A strange sensation stole over me, like I was falling and rising at the same time. Maybe she had such an effect on me because she expected more from me than I did, and it made me want to claw my way out of the selfish habits of my past to become a person who wouldn't disappoint her.

That was a strange thing to think, especially for me.

Her eyebrows drew together, forming a tiny wrinkle in the center of her forehead. I realized we'd stopped moving, the closed door to the secret office a dozen steps below us.

"Kit," she whispered. "What's wrong?"

Wrong? Nothing was wrong. I just couldn't look away from her eyes for some reason. My pulse beat loudly in my ears, and warmth spread from the center of my chest toward my toes.

I reached out, and her eyes widened when my fingers brushed across her cheek. I drifted closer and she inched away. Her back bumped the wall. She caught my wrist as I slid my fingers across her jaw and into her hair.

"Kit," she began.

That breathless note in her voice. It was music. It was a siren call—and I was Odysseus, bewitched and helpless.

She was still holding my wrist, but she didn't stop me when I wrapped my hand around the back of her neck. Her breath caught as I pressed into her. My other hand was on her waist, tugging her closer. Vaguely, I realized my actions were ridiculously inappropriate for this time and this place, but I couldn't stop myself.

She exhaled in a rush, drawing herself up, lips parting to speak.

I leaned down. Whatever she'd been about to say, it no longer mattered. Her eyes had gone wide again, face flushed, fingers squeezing my wrist—but not pulling my hand away. Not resisting as I tilted her head back.

Our mouths met. A soft kiss, heavy with anticipation, like we'd both been waiting for this moment for years—except we'd only known each other for days.

What the hell was wrong with me?

The thought fizzled in my mind, but my lips were already moving against hers. Her mouth had fascinated me since that first stern scowl in the interrogation room, and now those soft lips parted for my tongue. Our kiss deepened, and as she arched in my arms, I pulled her hard against me, my hand sliding up her back.

With a sudden gasp, she tore her mouth away. "Kit!"

"Hmm?"

"Stop."

"Why?"

"Because this isn't real. This is Quentin's power."

I blinked slowly. My thoughts were sluggish, hazed with desire. Wrapped in my arms, Lienna stared up at me, her cheeks flushed and chest rising and falling with each breath.

I wanted to kiss her again. I needed to. I couldn't focus on anything else, except …

Quentin. His name was like a black hole in my head, sucking in all the heat and passion clouding my thoughts. I knew his abilities. I knew what he could do. I knew how he could make you feel things that weren't real.

Things like an overwhelming desire to kiss Lienna while we were supposed to be stopping him from opening that vault.

I lurched back from her with a curse. "I'm so sorry. I didn't realize—"

"It's fine." Her gaze skittered across everything except me. "Are you back to normal?"

"Not even close."

Her alarmed stare darted to mine.

"Knowing it's him doesn't make me immune," I growled. "But it helps me resist. Why didn't you say something *before* I kissed you?"

Her mouth opened soundlessly—and her flush deepened. "I was caught off guard, okay? I can't feel whatever he's doing." She tugged her cat's eye pendant straight. "He must be down there. Let's get this done."

I pulled my shredded concentration together. Not easy when Quentin's love rays were pounding into my brain and I had to fight the urge to pull Lienna against me and—

Arg. I hated his power. I really did.

As we rushed down the final steps, I reapplied the invisibility warp, then created an illusion of the door so that when Lienna opened it, Quentin would have no idea.

Light flooded the stairwell as she drew the door open on silent hinges. And there he was.

My former best friend. My new enemy.

Quentin, his blond hair mussed and blue eyes bright, leaned against Rigel's desk, casual as could be. Maggie crouched in front of the Celtic knot etched in the floor, which I'd scarcely noticed during our first visit—except it was no longer an etching. A square of hardwood was missing, revealing a steel door set in the floor.

"Almost done, my love," she cooed, her curly blue ponytail bobbing as she fumbled with four vials of different colored liquid. "It will be ours soon. Very soon."

"And then we'll be safe," he purred back, and a shiver ran over my skin. Adoration, longing, desire, attraction, and sweet, sappy infatuation rolled off him in waves, bombarding Maggie's brain.

And mine.

Quentin was laying it on thick, ensuring Maggie stayed loyal to him until that vault was open. We had to stop him—but it wasn't as simple as charging in there, invisible, and punching him in his smug jaw.

A shimmering, semi-transparent bronze barrier filled the doorway, preventing anyone from entering the office. Despite its insubstantial glow, I knew better than to try to step through the magic.

"An alchemic barrier," Lienna whispered. "I can break it—I think. But"—she dug into her satchel—"I'll need a few minutes to do it."

"We don't have a few minutes," I hissed back as Maggie poured one of the four potions into a small divot in the vault's door.

"Then distract them!"

Right. I could do that.

Ensuring I had a firm grip on the invisibility and door warps, I conjured up my clearest memory of Rigel and projected my former boss into the office. He appeared behind the desk, unseen by the two would-be thieves, then conspicuously cleared his throat.

Maggie's head jerked up, and her mouth fell open. Quentin whirled, a shocked gasp rushing into his lungs, and the bombardment of loveyness fuzzing my brain disappeared.

Rigel gazed impassively at the trespassers, perfectly poised with his hands clasped behind his back, clean-shaven with his dark hair slicked to his head, and clad in his charcoal pinstripe suit.

"What are you doing here, Quentin?" I made him say, his crisp English accent emphasizing the tone he always used that suggested everyone in his presence was beneath his notice. "You wouldn't be trying to access my vault, would you?"

"Impossible!" Quentin stammered, his eyes wide and nostrils flaring. "You're dead!"

"I'm a man of many talents," Rigel stated simply. "Rising from the dead being one. Resisting the powerful gift of my favorite young empath being another."

Maggie frowned. A wave of gooey devotion hit me as Quentin realized he'd let his love-bomb falter.

I took a moment to glance at Lienna. She'd pulled a large pad of paper from her satchel, as well as a geometry kit and a calculator—not a pocket-sized one, but the big fat graph-making kind I remembered from high school algebra.

Refocusing on the office, I had Rigel raise an eyebrow mockingly. "Impressive work as always, Quentin. Submersing this young woman so deeply in feelings of affection until she became convinced the emotions were real—a delightful manipulation."

Quentin's jaw clenched, his sharp gaze jumping from Rigel to Maggie and back. She held her second potion vial above the vault door, motionless as confusion pinched her face.

"Yes," Rigel went on in a murmur. "You're unusually adept at making pretty women feel as though they're living out their own version of *The Notebook*."

Quentin's mouth dropped open—then he burst out laughing. "You almost had me! I almost believed it!"

Uh-oh.

I stole another glance at Lienna—now drawing a circle on her paper with a protractor—then had Rigel cross his arms. "Is there a problem?"

Quentin turned away from the projection, facing the doorway. "Come on out, Kit. I know it's you. Rigel never watched movies. He wouldn't know *The Notebook* from *Napoleon Dynamite*."

Aw, crap.

I made Rigel shake a finger at Quentin's back. "Death has given me a lot of time to binge-watch Netflix. I just finished the first season of *Riverdale*. I think they filmed part of an episode in this building."

Ignoring his dead boss, Quentin knelt beside Maggie. He caressed her cheek. "It's okay, love. It's just Kit messing with us."

"Kit is here?" She looked around. "Kit?"

Keeping Lienna invisible, I let all other warps die. Rigel and the fake door vanished, revealing me standing on the other side of the barrier.

"I'm here, Maggie. I came to help you."

Her eyes narrowed. "You betrayed me to the MPD."

On the word "betrayed," she poured the second potion into the waiting divot. Two out of four.

"I was never going to let them get you, Maggie," I explained urgently. "I wouldn't hurt you—but Quentin is hurting you right now. He's tricking you so you'll open that vault for him."

Quentin placed his hands on her shoulders and smirked at me. He was channeling that feeling of devoted love into Maggie at max output. I could feel the shock waves of emotion buffeting me, and I had to muster every iota of selfish, cold-hearted assholishness I possessed to counter the fluttery desire to throw myself at the nearest person and profess my undying love—which was Lienna, who'd already endured one "sappy Kit" experience.

I'd be embarrassed later. If we survived this.

Maggie uncorked the third bottle.

"Quentin's an *empath*," I reminded her, desperation creeping into my voice. "You know that, Maggie. You know what he can do. The love you feel for him isn't real. He's faking it."

She poured potion number three into the vault door. "You can't fake this."

"That's right, babe," Quentin crooned, rubbing her shoulders. "Stop trying to taint our love, Kit. We know you're only here because you want the artifact for yourself."

His sneer mocked me. I couldn't reach him, never mind stop him.

I glanced down. Lienna had drawn a complex geometric design and was frantically populating it with runes.

"Maggie, please listen to me." Yeah, I was begging. "Even if you love him, this is wrong. What about your speech about the evils of greed?"

She pulled the last cork. "I know what I'm doing."

Before I could try again to stop her, she upended the vial over the vault door. The gold liquid filled the final divot, and all four potions began to glow. Purple smoke wafted upward, drifting through the office.

"Lienna!" I hissed out of the corner of my mouth.

"I'm almost done! Almost—"

With a thick puff of smoke, the glow extinguished. A handle had appeared in the center of the heavy steel door.

"*Lienna!*"

Quentin reached for the door, and out of desperation, I conjured a snake on top of the handle. Quentin couldn't stand snakes. It was literally his only weakness, the asshole.

He jerked his hand back from my hissing serpent, then laughed—though I didn't miss the terse edge to the sound. Ignoring Maggie's surprised gasp at the hallucination, he looked up at me.

"Nice try, Kit."

He stuck his hand through the vision and grasped the handle. He heaved, and with a pneumatic puff, the door swung open on a silent hinge.

"Here!" Lienna leaped to her feet and slapped her paper against the bronze barrier blocking the doorway. "*Ori impero corrumpatur!*"

Azure light blazed over her arcane drawing, and the barrier collapsed like a waterfall. The substance was still splashing over the floor as Lienna and I leaped across the threshold.

Maggie scrambled backward, but Quentin's face split into a cold grin. With one hand reaching for the vault, he pulled the other from under his jacket. A black pistol glinted as he pointed it straight at me.

Without the slightest hesitation, he pulled the trigger.

The ear-splitting impact of the gunshot and the diaphragm-locking impact of the bullet hit me simultaneously, and an instant later, Lienna tackled me around the waist.

I slammed into the floor, and the third impact in as many seconds sent a burst of agony into my chest as if a red-hot steel rod had been rammed straight through my ribs. My left hand clamped against the burning hole in my torso and warm wetness squished between my fingers.

Lienna pressed both hands on top of mine, pushing down to slow the gush of blood.

"Kit!" Maggie gasped. "You—Quentin, you *shot him.*"

Smiling coldly, he took aim for my head.

"Quentin!" Maggie grabbed his sleeve. "Kit isn't—"

He tore his arm free—then smashed the butt of the gun into the side of her face. She crumpled with a high-pitched cry.

"Don't interfere!" His feverish stare snapped back to me. "And you two, don't move."

Keeping the gun trained on me and Lienna, he reached into the dark interior of the vault. When he withdrew his hand, he held a simple silver wand, its twelve-inch length etched with minuscule runes.

"Finally," he breathed, rising to his full height. "Blue Smoke wasn't just a plan to steal an artifact, you know. That was just the first part. Steal the artifact—then give it to *me.* And with my amplified power, we would have …" He glanced at me with a condescending sneer. "Ah, but that's way above your pay grade, Kit."

As much as I would've loved to make a cutting, witty retort, I couldn't get enough air to speak. Inhaling burned like hell, and the pain radiated across my body like a miniature nuclear bomb exploding inside my chest. Lienna pressed down on the bullet hole, unable to do anything else with that gun aimed at us.

"Tell you what, Kit," Quentin murmured. "I'll let you experience it before you die. Maybe the emotional overload will stop your heart." He raised the wand. "I've wondered, you know, if emotion can kill. Time to find out."

"Lienna!" I gasped soundlessly.

She shoved her hand into her satchel, fumbling for a weapon.

"*Ori meam incendo mentem.*" The words rushed off Quentin's tongue. "*Meam augeo potestatem, meum cor crescat!*"

A faint shimmer ran across the wand. For one naïve moment, I hoped the artifact had failed to activate.

Then my mind imploded.

Every emotion Quentin was experiencing hit me with impossible force, like an entire cargo ship of feelings cramming inside my skull—vindictive glee, burning triumph, and cold loathing for the weak, pathetic minds all around him that he could manipulate so easily.

Halfway through leaping toward him with an artifact from her satchel, Lienna collapsed, clutching her head. She was screaming. Maggie writhed on the floor, a shriek rising from her throat. I might've screamed too, if there'd been any air in my lungs.

Quentin watched them fall, laughing. An explosion of manic elation hit an instant later and a spasm shook my body, jarring the wound in my chest.

If there's one thing more powerful than emotion, it's pain.

My head cleared enough for conscious thought to pop back into gear. I dug my fingers into the bullet hole in my chest, and a fresh blade of agony pushed out the empath's supercharged emotions.

Lienna and Maggie gasped and shuddered on the floor. Quentin stood over them, laughing like a madman. I had to act, to do *something*, but I could barely breathe, let alone stand.

So, I did the only thing my emotion-logged, pain-hazed brain could think of. I created another snake.

The wand in Quentin's hand transformed into a thin, footlong silver serpent. It opened its tiny mouth, fangs extended, and hissed—the sound drowned out by Lienna's and Maggie's cries.

Quentin's fear slammed into me, followed by a wave of furious determination.

"Illusions!" he roared. "Hallucinations, Kit! Nothing you can do is real!"

"They're …" I gasped weakly. "… called … *warps*."

The silver snake spun around Quentin's wrist. With every ounce of concentration I possessed, I imagined its smooth, cool scales sliding over his skin. Imagined its thin, muscular body coiling around his forearm and constricting. I imagined the needle-like pierce of its fangs as it struck.

He screeched, panic exploding from him, and flung his arm out. The snake-wand flew across the office and clattered behind the sofa.

The emotional assault cut off like a pulled plug. I sagged against the floor, wheezing.

Quentin stared at his arm where the fake snake had bitten him, fear spilling out from his regular-strength empath abilities.

"No," he panted. "Impossible. You—"

He swung his gun toward me, and Lienna tackled him around the waist.

They slammed down and the pistol skidded across the floor. She drove her fist into his jaw, then tried to pin him, but he had at least fifty pounds of muscle on her. He threw Lienna off, lurched up, and kicked her in the stomach as she tried to roll away.

He lifted his foot to stomp on her head—and a blast of sound exploded in my ears.

Quentin staggered back. Two more gunshots tore through the room, and two more bloody holes appeared in his chest. He stumbled another step, hit the wall, and slid down, leaving a streak of blood across the paint.

Maggie knelt beside the desk, clutching his dropped gun in shaking hands. Her face was white as a ghost, but her jaw was clenched and her normally gentle eyes burned.

My vision doubled and blurred. I was gasping frantically but getting no air, and I realized vaguely that my lung had collapsed.

"Kit!"

Lienna leaned over me. Maggie appeared on my other side, tears in her eyes.

Their mouths moved, but I couldn't hear them over my desperate attempts to breathe. Their faces seemed to be descending into darkness. The room faded.

I slid into unconsciousness.

24

DOOM. That's what I felt.

Pure, unfiltered, one hundred percent naturally sourced, pulp-free doom. Raw, organic, free of antibiotics and pesticides. Freshly squeezed by the claw of the devil himself and served to me by the angel of death.

"It was nice knowing you," I whispered to Lienna. "I'll see you on the other side."

She rolled her eyes. "You'll be fine."

"Easy for you to say. You're not the one who's gonna be executed."

"They won't execute you, Kit."

Jangling the handcuff around my left wrist, the other end locked over the rail of my hospital bed, I didn't bother explaining that she had no way of knowing what would happen at my sentencing hearing. Which, big surprise, was still on despite my recent bout of do-gooder goodness.

When I'd turned down Vera's one-way cargo-ship cruise, I'd known my chances of escaping Vancouver a second time would be slim—and those odds had plummeted to zero the moment Quentin shot me.

Arrested was better than dead, though. Mostly.

A day after the whole chaotic showdown, I'd woken to find myself in the care of an MPD healer, with a pair of anti-magic handcuffs chaining me to my bed. Stopping Quentin had not won me any leeway with the MPD judicial system.

Joy.

My healer, Dr. Farnsley, was a portly man in his sixties. He reminded me of Danny Devito but without the boisterousness. He'd already repaired the worst of the damage caused by Quentin's well-aimed bullet—which had missed my heart by an inch—but nothing could insta-fix my lungs after their gruesome blood-drenching. I'd be stuck in this bed for a while yet.

Lienna had shown up two minutes ago, sat in the chair beside my bed, and promptly informed me that my sentencing hearing was still scheduled for next Thursday—a week from now.

"Do they even care that I helped stop Quentin while simultaneously taking down a gang of illegal artifact dealers?" I demanded indignantly.

"Of course." She pulled her legs up to sit cross-legged on the chair. She opened the fat folder she'd carried in with her. "But you could've helped without escaping custody and disappearing for three days."

"Are you *still* mad about that?"

She shot me a look that could flay flesh from bones. "I trusted you, and you ran away."

I tossed my head in a devil-may-care way. "I'm a psycho warper; it's what we do."

"You didn't know you were a psycho warper until yesterday!"

I arched my eyebrows. Her mouth twitched with the effort not to smile, then she dropped a magnificent eye roll on me.

Recovering her composure, she shuffled through a few pages in her folder. "Now that you mention it, I believe they added 'escaping custody' to your charges."

I swore under my breath. "So I just have to go in front of the Judiciary Council and beg for mercy, is that it?"

She pressed her lips together, all signs of humor gone.

"I'm looking at serious jail time, aren't I?" Or worse.

"It's hard to say, Kit. A lot will depend on what Captain Blythe has to say."

I swore again. "Well, do me a favor. When they throw me back in the clink, make sure I'm not cellmates with a lunatic serial killer, okay?"

"I'll see what I can do," she muttered, not sounding all that confident. I supposed that request was outside her jurisdiction as a field agent.

"What about my fellow criminals?" I asked, needing a topic change. "Did Faustus survive?"

"Alive, but we'll see what the Judiciary Council has to say about that."

Hmm. On one hand, I wasn't thrilled that Faustus Trivium was still walking this earth; I had no sympathy for that creepy hunk of shit. On the other hand, no burdens on my conscience.

"And ..." I hesitated. "Quentin?"

"Dead."

No surprise there. Maggie had put triple the number of holes in him than he'd put in me.

"Anyone else?" I asked, aiming for a casual tone.

"One of Faustus's men didn't survive his wounds. The Crow and Hammer team didn't hold back—not that they could in that situation."

"How about Eggsy? The crazy bastard was right in the thick of it."

"I think they scared him into signing an NDA, but Blythe isn't happy about a human having that much knowledge."

I settled more comfortably against my pillow and closed my eyes tiredly. "If she wants to keep an eye on him, the precinct has a lovely parking garage he could guard. It was ridiculously easy to sneak in there, by the way."

Lienna snorted.

Fatigue washed over me, and I felt myself drifting. Dread over my coming judiciary hearing had settled deep in my gut, but there was nothing I could do about it. I'd known before returning that this was the most likely outcome.

But I'd stopped Quentin and saved all the people he would've hurt with that artifact. I'd saved Maggie too—or … had I?

My eyes cracked open. "What about Maggie?"

Lienna looked up from her folder. "She's in custody. I think they scheduled her hearing for the same day as yours."

"What?" I burst out, triggering a spike of pain through my ribs. "Quentin was manipulating her! They can't punish her for that!"

"She was his willing accomplice." Lienna grimaced. "Textbook empaths aren't anywhere near as powerful as Quentin, so her sentence will depend on whether the Council believes he could've manipulated her to that extreme. I submitted a witness report explaining what I saw and experienced, but …"

She trailed off with a shrug—and a faint blush.

An odd twist disturbed my gut. Had her report included how, under the influence of Quentin's power, I'd pinned her to a wall and kissed her?

I opened my mouth—then closed it firmly. There was no need to mention how a predisposition toward an emotion made Quentin's abilities work all the better. And no need to question how I'd gone from "I'm gonna stop that empath bastard!" to "I'm gonna make out with Lienna in this dark, creepy stairwell!" in a matter of seconds. And definitely no need to ask why she'd taken so damn long to stop me.

That'd just be awkward, right?

My eyes drifted closed, thoughts lingering on that ill-timed kiss, which was emblazoned very clearly in my memory. My consciousness fizzled out as exhaustion took over.

"Kit?"

A gentle hand shook my arm, and I cracked my eyes open. Lienna was leaning over my bed, her satchel hanging off her shoulder. The blinds over the window, which last I looked had been open to let the afternoon sunlight into the room, were closed and the bedside lamp was on.

I carefully pushed up on my pillow, fighting back a yawn. "I fell asleep?"

"A few hours ago, yeah."

And she'd stayed with me anyway?

Before I could follow that thought to its sappy conclusion, she dug her hand into her bag. "I have to go, but first, I need to show you something."

She slid her hand from her bag and held out a strange metallic sculpture. It was a footlong silver snake, thin-bodied with delicate scales. The metal serpent was twisted in a coil, its tiny mouth open threateningly and fangs on display.

Pushing it into my non-cuffed hand, she watched me with an unusual degree of intensity as I examined the sculpture.

"It's kind of cool," I said uncertainly, "but not really my style. What is it?"

"It's the artifact from the vault. The silver wand."

I stared at the sculpture. "This can't be the wand."

"It is. I found it behind the sofa where Quentin threw it after you … after you turned it into a snake."

"I didn't turn it into a snake. I made Quentin *hallucinate* that it had become a snake. It was a warp."

She shook her head, still watching me carefully. "It's a snake now. It's not even an artifact anymore. Its magic is gone."

I didn't know what to say. An uncomfortable sensation built in my chest—an unsettling blend of disbelieving excitement and bone-deep terror.

I hastily set the sculpture on my blanket-covered lap like it might burn me. "So you're saying … with nothing but the power of my brain … I transformed a wand into a snake? A *real* snake?"

"A metal snake. But yes."

We stared at each other.

"But Lienna …" I rubbed my face. "My powers are visions and projections—unless this is something all psycho warpers can do?"

"Not in any of the documentation I've uncovered about psycho warping. You didn't warp someone's psyche. You warped—"

"—reality," I whispered, my gaze returning to the silver snake. "I warped *reality*."

And while those were the three coolest words I'd ever uttered in my life, they were also terrifying. All magic had rules. What were the rules of reality warping? Because that seemed like a really freakin' important thing to know before I started turning wands into snakes. Assuming I could do it again.

Lienna plucked the silver snake off my lap and stuffed it in her satchel. "My report on the incident … it doesn't include that you turned the artifact into something else. The artifact is officially missing from the crime scene."

My mouth fell open. Strait-laced, by-the-books, all-criminals-are-bad-people Agent Shen had lied in her report?

"Why?" I asked quietly.

She tucked her satchel against her side. "I don't think anyone should know about this power, Kit. Changing reality … that's the kind of thing that draws attention."

I read between the lines: the attention I'd draw would not be the good kind.

"Got it." I managed a weak smile. "I'll just keep that tidbit to myself."

Her smile was much warmer and more confident than mine. "In the meantime, I'll do some discreet research on reality warping."

"Okay." As she stepped back from the bed, I caught her wrist. "Lienna … thanks. For everything."

Her smile widened and softened simultaneously, and in a half-decent Bogart impression, she quoted, "Here's lookin' at you, kid."

Laughing, I watched her walk to the door. The latch snicked shut, and my amusement faded as I slumped into my pillow.

My gaze drifted to the cuffs around my wrist. As much as I wanted to know more about this newfound ability, depending on how my hearing went, I might never get the chance to test it again.

25

JUNE FOURTEENTH.

Eight thirty a.m.

My sentencing hearing had arrived.

I sat on a rock-hard plastic chair in a waiting area on the precinct's third floor, several levels above the holding-cell accommodations I'd previously enjoyed. Shiny handcuffs chained my wrists together in front of me, and I twisted and untwisted my fingers with fidgety apprehension.

Lienna sat beside me, hands resting in her lap and ankles primly crossed. She was ostensibly my magic-wielding, will-crush-your-bones-if-you-try-to-run escort, but she was also my moral support on one of the scariest days of my life.

She didn't know how much it meant to me that I wasn't sitting here alone, waiting for the literal gavel to fall.

According to the pleasantly bland old man running the desk at the head of the room, the Judiciary Council was already running behind because two of the six members hadn't shown up. They must have had tee times they couldn't reschedule.

I glanced around at the bizarre collection of mythic criminals. Their unfamiliar faces ranged from fear to anger to disinterest—except for one.

Maggie's blue hair drooped around her face as she stared at her lap, handcuffs shining against her gray jumpsuit. Her face was pale, her eyes puffy and red from crying. She sat alone. I'd tried several times to catch her eye, but she'd only looked at me once before fixing her stare on her lap again.

That one look had been full of shame and hurt and fear. Quentin had wrecked her, the bastard. Already paranoid Maggie would never trust again.

I forced my gaze away from her. It skidded across the room and back to the intake desk and the innocuous door beside it—the door behind which the Council would pass judgment on us.

Aside from Maggie, I'd spotted one other familiar face. My good ol' pal Duncan, the water-obsessed serial killer, had been walking through that door right as I'd arrived. He'd been in there for over twenty minutes now.

"What do you think will happen to him?" I whispered to Lienna. "Life in prison?"

"No, they'll definitely execute him."

"Right there *in the room?*"

She scoffed impatiently. "No. There's a short grace period—mainly for the paperwork. But there's no way he'll get anything less than the harshest sentence after all the people he killed."

"That doesn't make me feel a whole lot better about my—"

"Kit Morris!"

I jumped like Zorro had just stabbed me in the ass. Maggie glanced up, her dull gaze flicking to me.

The bland man behind the desk scanned the room, then called again, "Kit Morris!"

"That's you," Lienna whispered, nudging my arm. "Go, Kit."

I stood on numb legs. She gave me another encouraging nudge, but when I looked back, she wasn't quick enough to hide the tight anxiety in her face.

Shit. Lienna was scared for me too—and now I was *really* freaking out.

"I'll see you when it's over?" I mumbled, needing a light at the end of my sentencing tunnel, however weak it might be.

She managed a smile, and goddamn was it a beautiful one—wavering, lower lip trembling slightly, but with a determined set to her jaw. "I'll be waiting."

"Even if they're taking me back to the holding cells?"

"Especially then." She arched an eyebrow. "That's where I work. You won't be able to escape me."

"Aren't you heading back to LA now that Quentin is … not a problem?"

"*Kit Morris!*" the desk agent called impatiently.

"Captain Blythe offered me a promotion if I stayed," Lienna replied in a rush. "A big promotion."

"Are you taking it?"

"Maybe. Now get in there before you annoy them by being late!"

Oh crap. Not a good start. I sped across the room and answered a few simple questions to confirm my identity, then the agent directed me through the terrifying door beside his desk.

I stepped through, prepared for almost anything—except for the empty vestibule on the other side, its white walls broken by a second door directly ahead. The one I'd just walked through banged shut behind me, and when I glanced over my shoulder, I saw the door didn't have an interior handle. No going back.

Gulping down my stomach, I opened the second door and walked into the room beyond.

I'd hoped for, at the very least, one of those intimidating old courtrooms you see in movies. Or even more appropriate, a dark and ominous room with each member of the judiciary panel lit by a single, high-contrast light that obscured their faces.

Instead, it was a run-of-the-mill conference room, as cold and utilitarian as everything else in the precinct. A big plastic table filled most of the space, and a single empty chair waited in front of it. The four-panel members sat on the far side, facing me. A transcriptionist sat at a small desk in the corner.

One more person, planted in a chair at the butt end of the table with her back ramrod straight, had joined the party: Captain Blythe.

She didn't acknowledge my presence, and for some reason, she had an enormous stack of folders and papers in front of her. Did she go anywhere without them?

Each panel member was roughly eight thousand years old and looked more like a team of oversized gremlins than actual people. As I perched on the edge of the empty chair, they stared at me through their unkempt and untamed eyebrows with a level of sternness I had never experienced in my whole existence.

The angriest-looking gremlin cleared his throat, then read my name off a sheet of paper, followed by a case number and the entire list of charges against me. Lienna was right: they had added my escape to the total.

"Do you understand the charges you are facing, Mr. Morris?" Angry Gremlin asked.

"Mostly, but I'm not super clear on a few of them."

That, apparently, was not an issue, because his only response was, "You may now state your defense."

Holy forking shirtballs. That was it? "Defend yourself, ignorant plebeian"? How was this system fair?

With a deep breath, I began to speak.

"I was a member of the KCQ guild. You know, the all-psychic one full of shitty conmen and crooked lawyers. One of my fellow members was Quentin Bianchi. You know about him?"

Blythe shot me a "What the hell are you talking about *him* for?" look, but the gremlins answered me with blank stares. I'd assume that was a "no," then.

"He was the most powerful empath anyone, including our GM, had ever seen or heard of. He could affect half a shopping mall on a good day. Rigel would have him fill roomfuls of people with feelings of happy contentment until they'd sign literally anything the lawyers suggested."

I paused in case someone planned to ask what my role in those manipulations had been, but the gremlins said nothing.

"He could make grown men cry over cute cat gifs. Once, he made an elderly woman so angry she attacked her husband on a public street—all so he could get a restraining order against her. Long story that involved invalidating their prenup. Anyway."

My cuffs jingled as I nervously adjusted my hands. "What I'm getting at is that Quentin was a stronger empath than you can imagine. He was Rigel's trump card, and that's why Rigel went off the rails when Quentin was arrested."

I leaned forward in my seat, looking each panel member in the eye. "At some point today, a woman named Maggie Cook is going to take this seat. She's a sweet, caring woman who only ever did legal freelance work for KCQ. The charges against her are all because of Quentin—because he used his empath powers to manipulate her. He flooded her brain with emotions honed to control her for—for I'm not sure how long, but at least a week.

"I don't know how the MPD justice system works. I didn't even know what mythics were a year ago. But unless this system is even more broken than the human one, there's no way you can convict her when she was being manipulated by a powerful psychic. There's got to be *something* in your laws to protect people who fall victim to other mythics."

The female gremlin on the far right coughed delicately. "Mr. Morris, this time is provided for you to present *your* defense, not to defend another criminal."

"Maggie isn't a criminal!" Fury spiked through me, and I slammed my fists on the table. "What's wrong with you people? Maggie was manipulated! Do you punish people who are controlled by alchemic potions? Would you convict someone of property damage because a telekinetic threw them through a window?"

"Mr. Morris," she began again in the same tone, "this time is—"

"I'm defending her because no one else will!" I threw myself back in my chair. "What's the point in defending myself? There's nothing I can tell you that Captain Blythe doesn't already know."

The panel exchanged unreadable glances. Blythe watched me impassively.

Angry Gremlin tapped his pen on the paper. "Is that all you have to say in your defense, Mr. Morris?"

"Yeah," I growled, breathing hard through my nose. "That's it."

"Please return to the antechamber while we deliberate. You'll be summoned when we reach a verdict."

I shoved out of my chair and stormed back to the door. Inside the blank white vestibule, I paced in circles, but away from the gremlins' emotionless stares, my righteous fury was fading fast.

Despair crept in to replace it. Kid-me had barely survived one broken, unfair system. Adult-me wouldn't make it out of this new, bigger, just as broken and unfair system alive. But maybe my explanation of Quentin's powers would count for something when Maggie's turn came.

Minutes ticked by, and I continued pacing to escape the dread pooling inside me and squeezing my lungs.

The door to the conference room swung open. I whirled to face it, my heart blocking my airways.

Captain Blythe stepped into the vestibule, looking as terrifying and disappointed in every molecule of my existence as ever. She closed the door behind her.

"Did they reach a verdict?" I asked tersely.

"The charges against you are serious, Mr. Morris." Her laser stare bored into me. "However, I believe they can be attributed to your naivety and stupidity rather than perversity or malice."

I blinked. Uh, well … naivety and stupidity were better than perversity and malice, at least?

"I shared my opinion with the Judiciary Council and recommended leniency."

Hope sparked—only to die as she continued.

"However, the Council disagrees. They've found you guilty on all counts and are discussing your sentence."

"Guilty … on all counts?" I whispered, feeling faint. So much for half my charges failing to hold up in front of the Council.

She folded her arms. "I can't overrule a sentencing once it's been determined. So, Mr. Morris, you have approximately sixty seconds to decide."

"Decide what?"

"You will agree to commit your substantive abilities to this precinct as an employee of the Magicae Politiae Denuntiatores for a period of no less than seven years."

Uh … what?

"In exchange, you will plead guilty to an assortment of misdemeanors and be fined accordingly." She raised a single blond eyebrow. "I have the power to offer a plea bargain to a defendant at any point before official sentencing. That's my offer."

"You … you can *do* that?"

"Thirty seconds, Mr. Morris."

Shit. She was serious.

In another universe, one that didn't involve me facing down the Four Gremlins of My Apocalypse, I would have laughed in her face. Willfully subjugating myself to Blythe's iron fist for seven years sounded like a genuinely terrible idea.

But in light of the "guilty on all counts" thing, and whatever maximum sentence those power-drunk jerkoffs figured I deserved, it had a whole lot more appeal.

As an extra perk, if Lienna took Blythe's promotion offer, I would no longer be a rogue, criminal, or convict. I'd be her coworker. If that wasn't an upgrade, I didn't know what was.

A stunned grin broke across my face. "Sure, Cap! Count me in."

She smiled tightly—wow, had I ever seen her smile before?—and extended her hand. It took me half a second to realize she wanted a handshake. I grabbed her hand and shook it firmly, trying not to wince as she ground my knuckles together.

And that was it. I was a free man. Or, I was no longer MagiPol's prisoner. I was their employee.

I stared bemusedly at the captain. Lienna had warned me that Blythe could influence my future, but I hadn't guessed how much power she could wield to change my fate.

And now I belonged to her for the next seven years.

Not sure how I felt about that yet.

"Welcome to the MPD, Kit," she murmured, a sternly thoughtful note in her voice. "I'm looking forward to putting your unique magic to use."

I couldn't stop a small laugh from leaking through my teeth as I thought of the wand I'd somehow transformed into a silver snake.

She had no idea who she'd just hired.

ABOUT THE AUTHORS

ANNETTE MARIE is the author of YA urban fantasy series *Steel & Stone*, its prequel trilogy *Spell Weaver*, and romantic fantasy trilogy *Red Winter*.

Her first love is fantasy, but fast-paced adventures, bold heroines, and tantalizing forbidden romances are her guilty pleasures. She proudly admits she has a thing for dragons, and her editor has politely inquired as to whether she intends to include them in every book.

Annette lives in the frozen winter wasteland of Alberta, Canada (okay, it's not quite that bad) and shares her life with her husband and their furry minion of darkness—sorry, cat—Caesar. When not writing, she can be found elbow-deep in one art project or another while blissfully ignoring all adult responsibilities.

www.annettemarie.ca

ROB JACOBSEN is a Canadian writer, actor, and director, who has been in a few TV shows you might watch, had a few films in festivals you might have attended, and authored some stories you might have come across. He's hoping to accomplish plenty more by the time he inevitably dies surrounded by cats while watching reruns of Mr. Robot.

Currently, he is the Creative Director of Cave Puppet Films, as well as the co-author of the Guild Codex: Warped series with Annette Marie.

www.robjacobsen.ca

SPECIAL THANKS

Our thanks to Erich Merkel for sharing your exceptional expertise in Latin and Ancient Greek.

Any errors are the authors'.

The MPD has three roles: keep magic hidden, keep mythics under control, and don't screw up the first two.

Kit Morris is the wrong guy for the job on all counts—but for better or worse, this mind-warping psychic is the MPD's newest and most unlikely agent.

DISCOVER MORE BOOKS AT
www.guildcodex.ca

THE
GUILD CODEX
SPELLBOUND

Meet Tori. She's feisty. She's broke. She has a bit of an issue with running her mouth off. And she just landed a job at the local magic guild. Problem is, she's also 100% human. Oops.

Welcome to the Crow and Hammer.

DISCOVER MORE BOOKS AT
www.guildcodex.ca

STEEL & STONE

When everyone wants you dead, good help is hard to find.

The first rule for an apprentice Consul is *don't trust daemons*. But when Piper is framed for the theft of the deadly Sahar Stone, she ends up with two troublesome daemons as her only allies: Lyre, a hotter-than-hell incubus who isn't as harmless as he seems, and Ash, a draconian mercenary with a seriously bad reputation. Trusting them might be her biggest mistake yet.

GET THE COMPLETE SERIES
www.annettemarie.ca/steelandstone

SPELL WEAVER

The only thing more dangerous than the denizens of the Underworld ... is stealing from them.

As a daemon living in exile among humans, Clio has picked up some unique skills. But pilfering magic from the Underworld's deadliest spell weavers? Not so much. Unfortunately, that's exactly what she has to do to earn a ticket home.

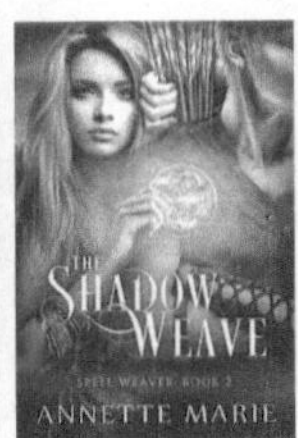

GET THE COMPLETE TRILOGY

www.annettemarie.ca/spellweaver

A destiny written by the gods. A fate forged by lies.

If Emi is sure of anything, it's that *kami*—the gods—are good, and *yokai*—the earth spirits—are evil. But when she saves the life of a fox shapeshifter, the truths of her world start to crumble. And the treachery of the gods runs deep.

This stunning trilogy features 30 full-page illustrations.

GET THE COMPLETE TRILOGY
www.annettemarie.ca/redwinter